COME
TO THE
RIVER

April Stinson Stubbs

ISBN 978-1-0980-2909-8 (paperback)
ISBN 978-1-0980-2910-4 (digital)

Christian Faith Publishing, Inc.
832 Park Avenue
Meadville, PA 16335
www.christianfaithpublishing.com

Printed in the United States of America

This book is dedicated to Don Stubbs, the love of my life. I praise God for the amazing, breathtaking summer of 1985. You were my knight in shining armor that rescued me from a life of black and white and brought me into a world of love, laughter and technicolor. Loveedoos my darling.

The evening sunset danced across the sky, transforming the raging muddy river into a blaze of color. Layers of burnished bronze, flamingo pink, mango orange, and hazy purple tumbled and sprayed in the churning current. Abby took her time walking the riverbank. She smiled as she looked at a swing tied to a high limb of a sycamore. Sweet memories came rushing back to her mind. She and her sister learned to swim and ski at a young age and spent many happy hours canoeing, fishing, and camping. Each season of the year, the river was rich in color and splendor. She remembered the winter the river had frozen solid. Practically the whole town came out to skate and build bonfires, but today the muddy river was ominous and made her feel uneasy with its powerful current.

Raising her arms overhead, Abby stretched and closed her eyes, enjoying the sun warm on her face. She was weary from working consecutive twelve-hour shifts as a home health nurse. Thankful to have the weekend off, she was looking forward to spending time with her church family here at the picnic. Pulled from her thoughts, she heard a man frantically shouting,

"Stop, Max, get back here. Stop!"

Abby turned to see who was shouting. Before she could react, a large black Lab barreled into her legs, tumbling her backward over the bank.

Isaac saw the dog racing toward the river, his leash dragging behind him. With horror, he saw the dog ram a woman into the water. Everyone ran to the bank, feeling helpless. People were shouting and pointing and crying out. With a running jump, Isaac vaulted into the water. He was a strong swimmer, but this river was treacherous.

It was all Abby could do to keep her head out of the water as she was swept into the tumultuous tide. She had absolutely no control trying to maneuver. Twice she had been able to kick and thrash hard enough to miss a boulder. She spotted a large fallen limb and knew if she didn't grab it, her chances of coming out alive were slim. Her strength was flagging. With a cry to God for help, she lunged herself at the branch. The rough wood scraped her tender flesh as she held on for dear life. The frenzied current was whipping her legs out of the water.

Abby inched her way along the limb, wrapping her legs around its base. With a loud crack, it flipped over, plunging her underwater. She pushed against it with all of her might. Her shirt caught, refusing to release her. She pulled and jerked with all her strength, panic clawing like talons at her throat. Her head was barely beneath the surface. Her eyes wide open, she could see sunlight spiraling rays of light through the murky water. Her arms shot out of the water, waving frantically. Her head felt like it would explode, pounding, demanding oxygen. Terror consumed her as the last bubbles of air escaped from her nose. Water ripped into her lungs, burning and gurgling.

Abby's limp body bobbed lifeless, her hair gently sweeping in the dark water. Suddenly the water stilled. In an instant, brilliant light shattered the darkness. Abby rose from the water effortlessly. She kept rising and continued high into the sky. She could see mountaintops, deep valleys, waterfalls, lakes, and rivers shining like mirrored glass. Her eyes drank in the beauty, taking in every detail of the vista. Never before had she such a keen awareness and appreciation for the exquisite splendor and magnificence of the earth. Never had she experienced such a revelation of God's love; that he had created the earth for her pleasure. She was filled with exhilarating awareness that Almighty God awaited her. She lifted her face to heaven. In the twinkling of an eye, she saw a portal open. Glorious colors emanated, reflecting from an inner light from heaven, colors she had never seen or experienced before, compelling colors filled with life and love. Dear familiar faces peered over the portal, smiling, beaming at her, waiting with eager anticipation. At once music filled her being. The music was alive and consuming. It was filled with God's love, in perfect blend and harmony. She could distinguish every instrument and every note in perfect precision. The music had life and depth and infinite, glorious praise. Rapturous joy filled her soul. She was reaching her arms out to her loved ones when her ascension abruptly halted.

At once, an aroma filled her senses. She closed her eyes and breathed deeply. The fragrance diffused and permeated, filled and satisfied. It was like completeness—like pure, rich, wholesome healing joy. Her entire being was filled to overflowing. She opened her eyes, and Jesus stood before her. She fell to her knees in worship, tears streaming from her eyes. He compelled her to rise. He gently cupped her chin and raised her face toward Him. When she looked into His eyes, His love swept through her like a hurricane. His eyes were breathtaking, holy, consuming like the depths of the ocean, vast and limitless. Light emanated from Him, for He was the light. His eyes bore into her. Love radiated from Him with intense adoration as if she had never sinned a day in her life. She glanced up at the portal. He nodded and smiled as He stretched His arm, causing the portal to roll back, allowing her a glimpse. In the distance, she saw lush mountains and waterfalls. The colors were vivid, and life pulsated from everything. There were amazing colors she had never seen on earth. She saw children and animals running and playing. There were people everywhere working with purpose and pleasure. There was order and great joy in serving. She laughed in delight as her eyes fell on a man working in a profusion of flowers. It was her Uncle James that had passed years before. His yard had always been the envy of the neighborhood. The portal closed. She heard someone calling out her name, pleading for her life. Others were interceding for her. She heard them boldly commanding for her life in the name of Jesus.

Isaac's strength was ebbing as he prayed for God to help him find her. The sun shot out behind the clouds and brightened the water just as he saw a hand beside a fallen limb. With long, forceful strokes, he swam toward her. He grabbed the limb with one arm and tried to pull her toward him. With herculean effort, he ripped her shirt free and wrapped his legs around her waist. Hand over hand, he inched his way along the log and, with his last ounce of strength, dragged them both to shore.

He laid her on her back and began CPR, counting compressions against her chest. His eyes never left her face as he prayed in the Holy Ghost. Giving mouth-to-mouth resuscitation, he pleaded for her life. Her lips were blue. That didn't stop him as he continued with supernatural strength from above. A cough, and water spewed from her throat. He turned her to her side, pounding her back as she expelled water from her lungs. Her eyes fluttered. With barely an audible voice, she whispered, "Jesus."

* * * * *

"Is everyone ready?" Rob, the brother of the bride, called as he knocked on the door.

"Yes, dear," called his mother, Kate. "We'll be ready in two minutes."

The bridesmaids were dressed in fall colors: burgundy, rust, amber gold, and olive green. Their dresses were long and A-line with a fitted bodice and three-quarter sleeves. Thankfully, it was a cool September day, perfect for an outdoor wedding at Stonehedge. The wedding was to take place at the amphitheater. The half-moon benches had been covered with white paper, and the center aisle had been thickly strewn with red rose petals. The bridesmaids got in line as the music started to play "Joyful, Joyful, We Adore Thee."

A lone flute played, and the sound carried over the forest with such an anointing that it brought tears to everyone's eyes. A guitar joined in, then a trumpet.

The flower girl was precious. Little Becca had on a white dress with embroidered flowers, and she was carrying a basket of white rose petals, delicately dropping them as she walked down the aisle. She had a very serious expression as she painstakingly dropped a petal with each step. Each bridesmaid carried a white Bible with satin ribbons to match their dress.

Catherine trembled slightly on her brother's arm. He covered her hand with gentle pressure.

"You okay, sis?" he whispered.

She nodded, trying not to cry.

Catherine looked up at the sky and whispered, "Daddy, can you see us?"

Her father, Charlie, had gone to be with the Lord eight months earlier. Cancer, that dreaded disease that caused them all such heartache. She felt his spirit with her as she began her descent. Her dress had been her mother's. Her mother had been a tiny young woman, but Catherine had little trouble fitting into the size 5 gown. The bodice was overlaid with lace, and the full skirt was covered with seed pearls and tiny hand-embroidered daisies, all white on white. The satin train was breathtaking, and the headpiece was made of magnolia blossoms and rich lace, cascading down her back. She was stunning. As they walked past their mother, they stopped as Catherine handed her mother a single white lily. Her father had given her mother a white lily on their wedding day forty-two years earlier. Catherine thought it fitting for her to be married on her parents' anniversary as a tribute to their wonderful marriage. The long stem had been wrapped with pearls and satin ribbon. Catherine and her mother embraced unhurriedly. Her mother, Kate, kissed her cheek and stepped back as they proceeded.

"Dearly beloved, we are gathered together in the sight of God, to join together this man and this woman in holy matrimony. Love is patient, love is kind. It does not envy, it does not boast, it is not proud. It is not rude, it is not self-seeking, it is not easily angered, it keeps no records of wrongs. Love does not delight in evil but rejoices with the truth. It always protects, always trusts, always helps, always perseveres."

Abby teared up as they recited their vows lovingly to each other. Abby was sincerely not jealous. She was thrilled for her dear friend and encouraged at their love for each other.

* * * * *

The reception was held at the outdoor pavilion at the Whipporwill Ranch with a live orchestra and wonderful food. The room was large with a huge fireplace at one end. There were twenty-five round tables that held eight chairs each. Each table was covered with a chocolate-brown tablecloth and a cream-colored satin sash overlay across the center. A beautiful centerpiece of blue and white hydrangeas sat in the middle of each table with a large candle under a hurricane glass.

Abby was headed for the ladies' room when she saw the flower girl skipping down the hall.

"Daddy, Daddy," she cried.

Abby turned, and her mouth dropped open as Isaac swung his daughter up in his arms. She hugged his neck as Isaac looked up to see Abby

"Well, hello," he said warmly.

Flustered, Abby stuttered a hello and ducked into the ladies' room. She hadn't been able to get him off her mind for weeks. Ever since the episode at the river, she had been thinking about him. She had even dreamed about him. She knew it was ridiculous to be embarrassed; nevertheless, she was. Her face flooded with heat as she looked at herself in the mirror. Today was the first day she had been out and about since the accident. She took her time before returning to the table. She stepped out of the bathroom and literally bumped into Isaac. Little Becca was nowhere in sight.

She looked up at him as he softly said, "Becca's my daughter."

"Yes, I assumed as much. She's beautiful," she said a bit too brightly.

"Yes, she is. She looks like her mother," said Isaac.

Abby didn't know how to respond. As she turned, Isaac reached out to take her hand. Startled, she didn't pull away; instead, she looked at him with guarded eyes.

"My wife died in childbirth four years ago, Abby. I haven't seen another woman since. I've thought about you daily since the river."

"Have you?"

He nodded yes. Abby noticed he still had her hand.

"I've wanted to call and check on you. I wanted to give you time to fully recover. Would you consider having coffee with me? I'd really like to talk with you."

"Yes, Isaac, I'd like that."

He said, "Could I have your number?"

Abby said, "Sure, do you want to write it down? I'll find something to write on," she said.

"Not necessary. Trust me, I'll remember it," said Isaac, smiling warmly into her eyes.

* * * * *

"Oh no, not again." Abby groaned as the other home health nurses held up the straws. "We have to draw straws again for Mr. Johnson? I just drew the short straw last week. It's not fair that I get it again. I should have immunity."

"No," said Jean. "It's the only fair system we could come up… the luck of the draw." The home health nurses were given a daily roster of duties each day. They checked on patients that needed care, and they also went into their homes to care for them. Most of the time, they dearly loved their job and grew very close to their patients. Occasionally, there were a few that were a real challenge.

Abby closed her eyes as she reached for the straw. She knew she'd drawn the short one as everyone burst out laughing. "Great, this is just great," she mumbled as she gathered her gear for the trek to Mr. Johnson's cabin up in the mountains. Mr. Johnson was an eighty-six-year-old black man that was bitter from an accident that left him crippled in a wheelchair. The only family he had left was a nephew that had nothing to do with him. The nurses hated going to his house because he was so snarly and combative.

Lord, I need Your grace today. Help me to show this man Your love. She got out of the car and slowly walked up his rutted driveway. Weeds had literally taken over the poor man's yard. The neglect of the place was evident. The house was dirty, and the kitchen was beyond dirty. She had offered many times to help him. He always swore and yelled at her, and she left in a hurry.

This particular day, Mr. Johnson was subdued. That immediately alarmed Abby. She took his blood pressure, a little low but pretty normal for him. Pulse, okay; respirations, okay; fever, 102.4.

She put her hand on his forehand, and he felt hot and dry. He rolled his eyes up at her, and for once, he didn't yell at her.

She said, "Mr. Johnson, have you had anything to eat today?"

"Nah, didn't want nuthin' much. Felt right rough this morning," he answered softly.

She said, "I want you to take a Tylenol and a glass of ice water. We need to bring this fever down." She began to assess him to see where the fever might be stemming from. He was sleepy and a bit disoriented. She started checking him over.

"Oh no, Mr. Johnson. It looks like you have a bad skin tear on your shin. I'm afraid it looks infected. Did you fall?"

He turned his eyes away and said with embarrassment, "I tripped on the steps."

Abby said, "You're going to need the doctor to look at this and get an antibiotic. Why don't you come on with me now, and I'll drive you down to the clinic."

"Nah," he said, "I ain't goin' nowheres. I be all right, miss. Go on now and tend to somebody that needs you. You ain't needed here."

Abby frowned and said, "I'll at least clean it and put on a dressing."

Mr. Johnson waved her away. "Nah, get on now."

Abby said, "But, Mr. Johnson, if you don't let me wash and dress that wound, it could make you sick very quickly."

"Now GIT," he yelled fiercely, startling Abby to the point she lost her balance and fell backward. Abby's pride was wounded more than her backside as she gathered her stethoscope and gear.

"Mr. Johnson, I'm going to ask you once again. Please let me treat your leg before I go."

"Nope," he said stubbornly.

Exasperated, Abby got back in her car and headed down the mountain.

* * * * *

Isaac smiled as his mind wandered back, reflecting on the course of events that led him to this beautiful Shenandoah Valley. Born in

Mississippi, his father had been the high school principal, and his mother had been a stay-at-home mom. After Isaac left home, she boldly announced she was finished raising children and wanted to get her driver's license. Then she shocked them all by going to work at Winn Dixie. She had been employee of the month four times in the last year, although the store manager had to have a chat with her about praying with people as she checked out their groceries. Too many customers would only let Mrs. Graham check them out even if they had to stand in a long line while other lines were wide open.

Isaac was the seventh child and the baby of the family. He had won a full athletic scholarship to the University of Mississippi. He had his heart set on being a high school coach. But after completing his first year, he had gone on a mission trip to Appalachia, and the poverty-stricken situations broke his heart. So many people had died senseless deaths because they couldn't afford basic health care. He sensed the Holy Spirit leading him to change his course for life, and he had switched his major to medicine. It hadn't been an easy road, but one that had given him a deep sense of satisfaction. He had met his precious wife, Rebecca James, in his last year of college. She had majored in nursing, and they quickly fell in love. She was an amazing woman with a beautiful spirit. Tall and willowy with long silky blonde hair and crystal blue eyes. They talked for hours about the ministry they felt God calling them to. She was the wind beneath his wings, encouraging him as he trudged through late nights and rounds at various hospitals during his internship.

God had blessed Isaac with a keen mind, and his professors urged him to start his own practice in a large city. He had been offered tremendous opportunities, but he turned them down knowing God had called him to practice at clinics to help the helpless. Many a time his professors became angry and called him a foolish waste of talent. Isaac stood strong in opposition.

He finished in the top five of his class and started his own practice in the hills of Kentucky. His patients paid him mostly with game and produce or trading work. The Lord always provided enough. Trading work came in mighty handy when his patients fixed his leaking roof and helped him shovel out during the big snowstorm last winter.

Sweet Rebecca wasn't materialistic, and they were happy with their humble home. When Rebecca became pregnant, they were both thrilled. As her due date approached, Rebecca had turned the tiny bedroom into a beautiful little nursery. She had made a pastel block quilt, and because they couldn't afford much, she took photographs of the neighbor's apple orchards in bloom and had them framed for the walls. A week before her due date, Rebecca started bleeding profusely. The umbilical cord was detaching from the wall. "Placenta previa," the OB doctor called it. They quickly did a C-section to try to save the baby, but a freak blood clot traveled, and Rebecca was dead. The baby lived. Rebecca died. In an instant, Isaac's world crumbled at his feet. As he held his newborn daughter, he looked down at the love of his life lying there like a crumpled flower. Tears dripped off his face as he clutched the newborn to his chest. He pulled back and studied her tiny features. She lay perfectly, still staring up at him with piercing blue eyes. She had a head full of blonde hair that puffed out like a baby chick. He handed her back to the waiting nurse and walked out of the room.

* * * * *

It seemed fitting that it should rain on the day of the funeral. Depression draped Isaac like weights as he stood under the funeral tent. Friends and neighbors patted him awkwardly, trying to say comforting words. It was useless; he was numb, and he was angry. His mother had come from Mississippi to help with the baby for a month till he could make plans. *Plans?* he thought. *That's a joke.*

Turning away, he slowly trudged in the mud back to his four-wheel drive. Seeing the baby car seat in the back jolted him back to reality. His anger changed to exhaustion as he drove back to the church. "Please, God," he prayed out loud, "help me get through this afternoon. I know these people have poured out their love to me with their flowers they can't afford and food they've prepared. Please help me to respond in kind."

The red numbers on the clock glared 2:20 a.m. as Becca was screaming her lungs out. Isaac stubbed his little toe hard on the corner of the coffee table as he stumbled into the kitchen to heat a bottle. As he lifted the baby out of the crib, her face was red, and her tiny fists were swinging in the air. "Okay, little one, settle down, Dad's here." The second the nipple went into her mouth, silence pervaded. Only the gulp and suck could be heard along with the gentle squeak of the rocking chair. Isaac softly hummed as he rocked. After her hunger had been satisfied, she yawned and nestled against him. "It's you and me, kid," he whispered. He fell asleep with her snuggled on his shoulder.

* * * * *

Abby sighed as her twin sister Andrea came out wearing her new pullover sweater. "Abby, can I borrow this?"

"Andi, it's brand new. I haven't even worn it yet."

"But you have plenty of clothes." Andi pouted.

Abby rolled her eyes as Andi ripped the price tag off. Abby knew she'd never see her sweater again.

Abby and Andi had been so close growing up. Mirror-image twins from birth. They had been the best of friends and had lots of fun fooling people as to who was who. They had been inseparable until their thirteenth summer. They were getting ready to go to church camp when Andi came down with the measles and couldn't go. Abby had given her heart to Jesus that week, and she couldn't wait to get home to share the experience with her best friend, but Andi wanted no part of it. It had put a wedge between them, which had broadened with each passing year. Abby had interceded for her sister until the tears fell on her feet, but Andi was adamant that she wanted no part of her religion.

Andi had made so many bad choices. Countless times, Abby had been accused and judged for things her sister had done. People would see Andi drunk and disorderly and assume it was Abby. She would have liked to have moved to another city to get away from her, but Andi was her sister, and Abby loved her deeply.

Andi worked as a bartender. She dropped out of college and seemed hell-bent on destruction. Her parents and others had talked to her until they were blue in the face about her potential and changing her life for the better. The more they talked, the more rebellious she became. In her early years, Andi had dreams of becoming a schoolteacher. She was smart and beautiful. Andi was a flirt, and she had honed it to a fine skill. She had so many relationships that Abby worried that she would get an incurable disease. Andi had an ace in the hole, and that ace was a praying grandmother. Her Mamaw loved her fiercely, and that woman knew how to pray. She had prayed for her granddaughters every day of their life. And she wasn't going to stop as long as she could draw a breath.

Andi's heart was tender when it came to her grandparents. She had wonderful memories of her grandparents' farm. She loved to spend the night. Her grandmother played "hide the button" with her and Abby. It was a simple game. Mamaw would pretend to hide a button somewhere in the room, and the girls had to guess where it was hidden. They got to wear Mamaw's nightgowns, and all slept together until they were too big to fit in the bed. She loved the sound of the rain hitting the tin roof and the smell of gingerbread baking. Papaw had taught her and Abby how to swim in the creek behind the house, and they had learned to ice-skate on the lake in the back field. They loved gathering eggs from the henhouse in the mornings. Mamaw had taught them how to make muffins, and Papaw had taught them how to break bottles with a homemade slingshot and, best of all, learning to ride Polly. She was so proud when Papaw let her take the horse out by herself for the first time. She thought of the "leaf quilt" she and Abby had made for Mamaw for her birthday. They scoured the woods picking out the most perfect, beautiful fall leaves they could find, all colors, gently placing them in a trash bag. They laid them out carefully under the big oak tree in the front yard, each leaf tucked carefully by the next one, building a full-length "quilt blanket." When they finished, they ran inside excitedly, shouting for Mamaw to close her eyes for her surprise. They led her out, carefully walking down each step. When she got to the tree, they yelled, "Happy Birthday, Mamaw! Open your eyes." Mamaw Esther cried at the painstakingly beautiful job they had done and took a photograph, which was still hanging in her living room.

Andi never felt judged by her grandparents, only cherished. Her Mamaw and Papaw had never spanked her even though she knew she needed it. Their form of punishment was to make her memorize scripture. They were so proud of her when she memorized it that Andi secretly enjoyed it just to please them.

She still recalled some of her childhood memory verses: "I will hide Your Word in my heart that I might not sin against Thee" (Psalm 119:11). And "The Lord is my refuge in times of trouble" (Psalm 9:9).

Andi hadn't seen her grandparents for two years. She refused to visit them. Her shame was too great. She knew her grandmother was praying for her, and she was fighting it with everything in her.

Andi could drink any man under the table. She liked the way the liquor felt burning down her throat. And she loved how it made her feel numb. Many a night, she awakened from a nightmare of a baby crying from the grave. Her past mistakes haunted her. No one could judge her more harshly than herself. Her good friend Jack Daniels could wash the pain away, at least for a while.

* * * * *

Jeremiah Graham did not like to fly; however, it beat driving in a car for hundreds of miles. He looked out the window at the clouds as he prayed for his son. "Lord, I know you have given me a word for my son. Prepare his heart to receive it." Jeremiah, or "Miya," as most people referred to him, was a strong man of God. He was a quiet man—a man of strength and character. He carried the mantle of a prophet, a gift that was hard to swallow at times. God was God and when He gave him a word he had to deliver it. Miya felt God speak to his heart to tell Isaac to move to Virginia. Miya had never been to Virginia and knew no one who lived there. He knew God had a plan for his son and granddaughter Becca. Miya smiled as he thought of his blonde beauty. Little Becca was quite the charmer. She was always happy, loved to skip and sing, and was a genuine beauty. She wasn't a bit afraid of snakes or grasshoppers. She loved animals. "When I am big, Poppy, I am going to be a doctor like Daddy. I will be an animal doctor for cats and cows and mice and chickens and puppies and goats," she said very seriously.

The overhead speaker announced the approaching descent and landing. Miya was looking forward to stretching his long legs.

* * * * *

Isaac was holding Becca as he strode through the airport. He spotted his father immediately as his dad stood six feet four. Even at age seventy-eight, his father stood tall and proud. Isaac whistled his special whistle that only he and his dad knew down through the corridor, and his dad instantly smiled and whistled back even though he couldn't see through the throngs of people.

"Poppy, Poppy!" cried Becca as she leaped from Isaac's arms into Miya's. She was strangling his neck with a hug while kissing him all over his face.

Miya laughed and said, "How's my bootsie girl?" as he held her up over his head.

Becca squealed with delight and said, "I can see really good up here, Poppy."

"Hello, son," Miya said with love in his eyes and voice.

Isaac hugged him and said, "Dad, you look great. How's Mom?"

"She is fine, son. She sends her love."

Isaac said, "Come on, Dad. Let's get you out of here."

They rode in comfortable silence up the mountain. The modest house was a small two-bedroom cream-colored stucco set back in the woods. It had a green tin roof with a large oak tree with a swing in the front yard. Isaac grabbed Miya's suitcase, and Miya carried a sleeping Becca into the house. Miya laid Becca on the sofa and looked around. Everything was clean—just a bit messy and definitely needed a woman's touch. Toys were strewn here and there. The kitchen was clean, but no frills. Miya laughed as he compared his son's kitchen to his wife's. The shelves on each side of the sink had a large tin of black pepper on one side and a box of garlic salt on the other. There were no curtains at the windows, but there were no neighbors, so it didn't really matter.

The living room had a sofa, a rocking chair, and a writing desk. A large oval rug covered most of the floor. There were no pictures on the walls. The bedroom had a bed and two dressers. The bed wasn't made, and there were some clothes on the floor and dresser.

Becca's room was painted pale pink. Her twin bed had a quilt, and on the wall were framed pictures of apple trees in bloom. There were lots and lots of stuffed animals. This room seemed a sanctuary in this masculine home.

"How about some lunch, Dad? I can you fix you the blue-plate special—a fried bologna and tomato sandwich, a grilled cheese, or some chicken noodle soup? What's your pleasure?"

Miya laughed and said, "A fried bologna sandwich sounds good, son. Your mother won't let me eat that kind of food. This will be a real treat."

After lunch, they were sitting on the front porch when Isaac said, "Okay, Dad, out with it. I know you well enough to know you didn't fly here just to visit. What's on your mind?"

"Son, the Lord gave me a Word for you."

Isaac braced himself. God had been dealing with him for months about change. He knew change was coming, and frankly he dreaded it. He had been playing games and trying to play dumb. Not that he didn't want to obey God; he had gotten so very comfortable here. He knew all his neighbors. He loved his church. Becca was happy. His practice was predictable. He was satisfied with his life. He had not been on one date since Rebecca passed. He could imagine his life just fine right here for a very long time.

Isaac listened intently as his father shared a story. While interceding for him one evening, the Lord had told him to deliver the message in person that God was calling Isaac to move his practice to the Shenandoah Valley of Virginia. Isaac felt shock shudder through him. To think…his father actually booked a flight (when he hated to fly) to come all the way to Oneida, Kentucky, to deliver this word. Isaac knew better than to ask questions. When the Lord gave a word to his Dad, he delivered the word intact. No more and no less.

* * * * *

Isaac rented a car at the Washington/Dulles airport and headed for Marion Gap, Virginia. He knew absolutely nothing about this town other than when he had been praying, Marion Gap was the name of the town the Lord had laid on his heart. He googled it and found it to be a very small town. Easily accessible and quite charming. The pianist at his church was delighted to watch Becca for a few days while he went to check out the lay of the land. He had an appointment with the top-selling realtor of that area at 1:00 p.m., so he had time to scout and stop for a bite to eat.

It sure is easy on the eye, Lord. I'll give You that. Isaac was driving and feasting his eyes on the green rolling hills and blue sky. He spotted a road sign, "The Lunch Box," and pulled into a small restaurant. White rockers were across the front porch with planters of flowers. The interior was spic and span. He took a booth and looked over the simple menu. He ordered the "special," a hot roast beef sandwich with mashed potatoes, gravy, green beans, and sweet tea with a piece of homemade pecan pie for dessert.

Just as he finished, he heard the bell tinkle over the door, and the real estate agent came bustling in. She was a big lady with big hair and a big smile. "Hey, Ralph. Hey, Theta," she said as she walked by the first table. "Eddie, you tell your mama I'll be by to see her after church tomorrow. And I'm bringing her some potato soup and a tape of the service." She evidently knew everyone in the restaurant, and they knew her. That sat well with Isaac. He loved small-town hospitality.

"Hey there, you must be Isaac Graham. I'm Betsy Brown, but everybody calls me Beebee. I have two homes to show you today that I think will fit your needs. Are you sure it has to be in the Gap? I know of plenty of places in the surrounding area, but there are only two right now in the Gap that meet your criteria. And I assume you have a four-wheel drive? That elevation can be tricky come winter. Have you finished eatin', darlin'? I don't want to rush you."

Isaac smiled and said, "Thank you, Beebee. I'm finished."

The first house had been a fine place, just needed a bit of handyman work. Isaac wasn't afraid of hard work, but the second one captured his heart immediately. The front living-room window had a spectacular view overlooking the valley. The backyard was green and lush, and there was a salt block in the rear of the property for deer. It had three bedrooms, two bathrooms, a large eat in kitchen, and a large living room with a vaulted ceiling. He knew this was the home for him and Becca. Beebee peppered him with questions, but he remained distant. She had wheedled out of him that he was a doctor. As it turned out, she wasn't just a nosy gal after all. She was actually a great networker. He told her he wanted to work at the health clinic, and she immediately produced a business card of whom to call.

"You just call Alex Berger. Tell him Beebee gave you the number. Son, I think you might be an answer to prayer in this town. The town clinic has been in dire straits for a doctor for the last five months, and all the doctors in town have been rotating turns to help out in the interim. You sure you don't want your own practice? I'm sure you'd be successful. Being a clinic doctor takes a special call with all the home health in the hills and all the indigent needs. That's more like ministry than a job, son."

Isaac smiled at her and impulsively kissed her cheek. "Thank you, Beebee. You've been very helpful to me."

Isaac drove through town with his mind racing. It would make a wonderful place to raise Becca. The valley was beautiful with the Shenandoah River flowing through it. He found his way down to the boat landing. He needed to be near the river to calm his mind. He rolled down the windows and closed his eyes. The sound of the water flowing over the dam settled his spirit. He flipped open his cell phone and dialed Alex Berger's number. His secretary answered, and in short order, he was introducing himself. They made an appointment to meet Monday morning at ten thirty. Isaac drove until he found a hotel with a pool and checked in. He needed some exercise, and some laps in the pool were calling his name. He was in the mood for a good steak and a good bed. Tomorrow he'd find a church service to attend, and hopefully he could get things in motion so he could get home to Becca.

* * * * *

"I think it's outrageous that he's going to uproot Becca without even consulting with us first," said Louise.

Jerry sighed at the tone of his wife. He knew she would make trouble no matter what he said. Ever since Rebecca died in childbirth, her mother, Louise, had been bitter toward Isaac and bitter toward God. She blamed Isaac. He was a doctor. He should have been able to stop the bleeding. If they hadn't lived in those God-forsaken hills of Kentucky, they would have been closer to a decent hospital.

"And I never get to see my grandbaby. Even when we do manage to get out visiting, he won't let me spend any quality time with her. The nerve of that hypocrite telling me not to plant negative thoughts in her mind. Who does he think he is? Now they're moving to Virginia, even farther away. Well, you can run, Isaac Graham, but you can't hide. We'll just see what the courts have to say about grandparent visitation rights!"

* * * * *

Isaac could hear the praise and worship band as he got out of his car at Living Water Fellowship. He slipped into the back row just in time to hear the pastor ask a woman named Abby to come and sing. The pianist played an intro, and she started singing "We Shall Behold Him." Isaac sat spellbound watching and listening. There were about three hundred people in attendance, and they had a small section for the deaf. Isaac glanced back as Abby started signing the chorus, "We shall behold Him, we shall behold Him, face-to-face in all of His glory." She smiled as she sang. Her sign-language skills were graceful, and Isaac was mesmerized. When she finished, the church jumped to their feet and began to clap. Isaac had never seen anything like it. The people were shouting and jumping and clapping. "There's power in praise," shouted the pastor. Isaac joined in and got lost in his praise to God.

Isaac's eyes traveled around the church. The ceilings were high with large windows down the side walls. There were beautiful tapestry hangings with scripture. Something the pastor was saying suddenly caught Isaac's attention. "I had an appointment last week and was running late. It was an important meeting and imperative for me to be on time. I was purposely speeding. I'm not proud of that fact. I had the pedal to the metal. I was passing cars left and right. Suddenly up ahead, I saw a state trooper. Guess what my reaction was?"

Everyone laughed at this point.

He continued, "My reaction was to jerk my foot off that accelerator. As I was praying and studying for today's message, the Lord brought that incident back to my mind. I had passed other cars on that highway that morning. They had no effect on me. However, when I saw the state trooper's car, I responded immediately. Why did I do that? It was because I understood the authority that car represented. We have authority as believers in Jesus Christ. Jesus has given us His name, and we can use that name knowing who we are in Christ. We have that same authority. Are you using your authority?"

Isaac meditated on Pastor Bob's message throughout the day. There were situations in his life where he should be using his authority. Isaac leafed through the visitor packet that listed the various ministries within the church. They seemed to have a great children's ministry and even had a Christian school.

* * * * *

Isaac's smile was a mile wide as he shook Alex Berger's hand.

"Welcome aboard, Dr. Graham. Your start date will be September 5, the day after Labor Day. Have you found a place in the area yet?"

Isaac answered, "Yes, I have. Betsy Brown was a tremendous help to me. Just this morning, I signed a contract for a house in the Gap."

Alex laughed. "That Beebee's something else, isn't she? She's a great little gal. I look forward to working with you. Please feel free to call me if you need anything, and I'll talk to you soon."

Isaac was walking on air as he went back to the car. *Well, Lord, looks like You've brought it all together.* He could hardly wait to call his dad and get moved and settled.

* * * * *

Louise slammed the phone down, muttering that all lawyers were liars and thieves. Jerry ignored her as he ate his lunch in silence.

"That's the third attorney that I've called that won't help me with visitation rights. I'll go to the Supreme Court if I have to."

Jerry felt his blood pressure rise. He had had his belly full of his wife's ranting and raving. He sat down his glass of iced tea and said in a steely calm voice, "Louise, I want you to see a doctor."

She started yelling at him when he stood up and backed her into the wall. She was so shocked that she actually fell silent.

"I've had enough, do you understand me? You refuse counseling from our pastor. This bitterness and unforgiveness have driven you mad. Maybe you need medication to help you, but I'll tell you one thing, and you'd better hear me and hear me well. I am sick to death of you acting like this."

Louise didn't open her mouth as Jerry walked out of the room. But her mind was racing a hundred miles an hour.

* * * * *

Abby knocked on her supervisor's door as she held the list of home health patients she needed to visit that day. It was absolutely unfair that she had to see Mr. Johnson again. She had seen him two weeks in a row and five times in the last two months. Drawing straws was no way to solve this dilemma.

"Come in," said Pat Whited.

Abby stepped in, ready to lay it on the line, but her boldness left her as Pat told her to be seated.

"Is there a problem, Abby?"

Abby cleared her throat and said, "Uh, well, not exactly. Well, actually, yes…yes, there is. You see, I've gotten Mr. Johnson on my rotation five times in the last eight weeks, and I was hoping another nurse could go today."

Pat raised her eyebrows and said, "Why did you get sent to Mr. Johnson's five weeks out of eight?"

Abby suddenly felt very childish. She didn't want her supervisor to know they drew straws to see who would have to go see him.

Pat said, "I'm waiting, Abby. I make up the rotation schedule, and I know for a fact I didn't assign you this patient that many times."

Abby said, "We—that is, the nurses and I—sometimes trade each other, and, well, Mr. Johnson is a bit of a challenge at times, and sometimes we draw straws. I'm sorry, Mrs. Whited. I know how unprofessional this must sound. I'll be on my way now. I'm sorry I bothered you."

"Just a moment please. You draw straws?" Mrs. Whited asked with a stone face.

Abby held her breath, not knowing whether Mrs. Whited would laugh or get angry.

"I see. If drawing straws has worked for you thus far, then I'm sure you don't need my help to work out this problem. Good day, Ms. Alexander."

Abby had never felt so humiliated in her life. "Lord, it serves me right. That'll probably blow any chance of a promotion. Looks like Mr. Johnson is my lot in life!"

* * * * *

Abby pulled into Mr. Johnson's driveway and was surprised to see an SUV parked there. She knocked on the door as she turned the doorknob and stepped in. That same stale smell hit her in the face. She heard a low bass voice speaking. She stepped back to Mr. Johnson's bedroom and was shocked speechless to see Isaac leaning over Mr. Johnson's bed. He was wearing a white jacket with a stethoscope around his neck. He looked up and paused at the look on her face. Abby looked from Isaac to Mr. Johnson. Mr. Johnson looked gray and was burning with fever. Her heart filled with compassion for him as she quickly went to his side.

"Mr. Johnson, it's Abby. How are you feeling?" His eyes were glazed, and he didn't respond.

"Can you call 911, Abby? He needs to be admitted."

"Yes, of course," she said automatically. She walked into the living room and called for an ambulance.

Isaac walked in and said, "I'm sorry if I surprised you."

Abby realized how little she knew about this man. She stared at him and said, "I didn't know you were a doctor."

"We haven't really had a chance to talk yet. I'm a general practitioner, and I work at the community clinic. We'll talk later, okay?"

Abby nodded, still groping for words, when he went back into Mr. Johnson's room.

* * * * *

Andi stared at the EPT test in disbelief. It was pink. She blinked her eyes and squinted against the bathroom light.

"Nooo!" she screamed as she slammed the test against the bathroom wall.

"I'm not waiting another day," she seethed. "I'll go to the clinic today and get this taken care of." She hardened her heart as she turned on the shower.

Isaac flipped open the chart outside the door of his next patient.

A. Alexander, female, age 29
Positive pregnancy test, scheduled for abortion.
Two prior abortions.
Currently taking Ortho-Novum birth control

Isaac would not sanction abortion, but when a patient insisted, he simply referred them to another physician. He eased open the door and jerked to a halt as he saw Abby lying on the exam table. Her face was turned to the wall. There was no mistaking her. He quickly stepped back and shut the door. He felt himself tremble. He walked back into his office and shut the door. He sat down hard at his desk, staring at the wall. *Lord, am I seeing things? Does Abby lead a double life? I'm speechless and so disappointed. I really thought we could develop a relationship. She was singing in church Sunday and knew sign language and was educated. What in the world is going on here?*

He stepped over to his colleague's office and knocked. "Dr. Davis, would you mind taking this next patient?"

Dr. Davis said, "Sure, no problem."

Isaac said, "Thanks, I owe you one."

* * * * *

Abby looked at the clock again as she finally accepted that Isaac was not going to call. She sighed as she prepared to pop some popcorn and watch her favorite Cary Grant movie. She had seen it so many times she practically knew the script by heart. It was her comfort movie, and she needed some comforting tonight. The smell of salty popcorn filled the air. She poured a glass of iced tea and settled into her favorite chair.

* * * * *

Sunday morning, Abby was watching for Isaac from the front of the church. She finally saw him come in a few minutes late and sit on the last row. Right after church, she slipped back so she could to speak to him. She tried hard to not look conspicuous, but by the time she weaved back, he was nowhere in sight.

The next day, Abby was at Morning Side Assisted Living Facility. She was helping Mrs. Forbes move from her bed to the bedside commode when she strained her back. The pain was so bad on the way home she could barely stand it. She had one last stop to make at the community clinic before she could head home. She walked in a little stooped over and checked in with the receptionist.

"What's wrong, Abby? Are you in pain?" asked Ginger.

Isaac was walking down the hall when he spotted her. He stopped before she saw him.

"Yes, I'm in so much pain."

Ginger said, "Dr. Graham's still here. Would you like him to take a quick look at you?"

Abby said, "No, no, I'm okay. I'm going home right after this. I have some pain pills left that Dr. Davis gave me."

Isaac was shocked. *She must have had that abortion last week. I was really looking forward to getting to know her.* He shook his head in disappointment as he walked back to his office.

The following Sunday, Abby stood in the back, purposely waiting for Isaac. He came in holding Becca's hand. As he slid in the pew, Abby stepped in beside him. She knew she was being bold. Yet she could care less because she was feeling desperate to talk with him.

"Hi," she whispered as she smiled up at him. "Is Becca over her chickenpox?"

Becca heard her name and leaned around and smiled at Abby. She still had some pox marks on her face and arms.

"She's better," he said without looking at her. He didn't try to engage in any more conversation. Feeling awkward, Abby slipped out of the pew after a few minutes of silence.

* * * * *

Isaac's pager went off at 12:25 a.m. He called the hospital to find one of the clinic patients was hemorrhaging. He quickly dressed and wrapped a blanket around Becca. Thankfully, he'd found a great babysitter for emergencies right here in the Gap. He gave her a quick call, and Linda met him at the door as he handed her his precious bundle.

"I'll be back as quick as I can."

"Take your time, Dr. Graham, we'll be fine," said Linda.

Isaac went into the hospital to see Abby lying on the table. He was flabbergasted. He knew he couldn't be unprofessional. He simply did not want to treat this woman.

The head nurse came up briskly and said, "The patient's name is Andrea Alexander, age 29. She's pregnant and hemorrhaging. We just drew blood to check her levels. She may be having a miscarriage. We have to wait and see."

Isaac was so rattled he didn't realize she said *Andrea* instead of *Abby*. He looked at her chart and was completely shocked at the sordid background of her medical history. Andi was softly moaning when he walked up to assess her. When she turned her face toward him and he looked into her eyes, Isaac nearly fainted. This was not Abby. He grabbed the chart and looked at the name again. It had to be her twin sister. Abby hadn't mentioned having a sister. But he realized he barely knew Abby. He silently prayed for forgiveness for judging Abby and jumping to conclusions.

Several hours later, Andi opened her eyes to see Dr. Graham checking her IV.

"Am I having a miscarriage, Doctor?" she asked.

Isaac said, "No, you're not, Miss Alexander. You did have some heavy bleeding, but the heartbeat is strong. This baby's a fighter."

As he walked off, Andi felt a moment of protection for her baby. She tried to shake it off when a scripture suddenly came to her mind: "Before I formed you in the womb I knew you; Before you were born I sanctified you" (Jeremiah 1:5). She placed her hand on her stomach, wondering what in world she would do. *I can't have a baby*, she thought. *I don't have a decent job. Oh God*, she whispered. It was as close to a prayer as she had ever prayed.

* * * * *

Abby heard that Andi was in the hospital. There was a large networking between hospital and home health nurses, and news traveled fast. Abby knew it was probably futile, but she still wanted to see her sister. She pulled into the hospital parking lot, praying that God would soften her sister's heart.

Andi's door was partially opened, and Abby could see her sitting in bed, looking out the window. She knocked softly on the door and called out, "Sis, can I come in?"

Andi looked over and smiled a sad smile when Abby walked in holding a white bear with a polka-dot ribbon around its neck. Their mother had given them twin bears as birthday gifts on their seventh birthday, and they had slept with them up to their teen years. Abby's had a red ribbon, and Andi's a polka-dotted one. Abby had seen the bear at Hallmark and shopped for the polka-dot ribbon, hoping it would bless Andi's heart. Andi hugged the bear and tried not to cry. Abby sat in a chair next to the bed and took her hand.

Andi said, "Please, Abby, no sermons today."

Abby said, "I didn't come to preach. I came to check on you and make sure you're all right."

"Right as rain," said Andi. They smiled at each other as they remembered their Mamaw always said that.

"Do Mom and Daddy know you're in here?" asked Abby.

"No, and please don't call them. I get released in the morning. Please, Abby, promise not to tell them."

"Okay," said Abby. "But, Andi, they just love you. They want to be there for you."

"I know that. I haven't decided what to do yet, and it will just create more heartache for everyone. I'm pregnant, Abby."

Abby squeezed her hand. "I'll help you with the baby, Andi. You know I will."

Andi turned her head and sighed. "I'd make a lousy mother, and you know it. I don't think I can do this."

Abby knew better than to say anything. She reached over and smoothed Andi's hair behind her ear and said, "I'm always here for you, Andi."

They sat quietly a few minutes when Andi said, "I'm a big embarrassment to Mom."

Abby said, "Don't say that, Andi. She loves you."

Andi rolled her eyes and said, "I didn't say she didn't love me, Abby. I said I embarrass her, and you know it's true. She throws it up in my face enough. She thinks what I do is a reflection on her. Her precious pride has always been her downfall. She's totally blind to that. You're the good daughter, I'm the bad daughter, and I've been a thorn in her side since we were kids. I don't resent you, Abby. I just wish she could accept me like I am. She can't. Those are her issues. God knows I have plenty of my own. It doesn't change the fact that she holds me at arm's length. So whatever! I don't know that I blame her. I'm a failure and have ruined my life and driven the family crazy. I'd be better off dead."

A tear slid silently down Andi's cheek as she squeezed her sister's hand.

Abby took a deep breath and boldly said, "You think I'm good? It's not me. It's Jesus."

Andi put her hand up and said, "Please Abby, don't."

Abby said, "Fine. I won't say anything else right now, but I am praying for you whether you like it or not." Abby desperately wished she and Andi were closer. Andi was closed off and hurting. Today she seemed a little more vulnerable. They sat content just to be together.

"I have to go to work, but you know where I am if you need me." Abby held her arms out for a hug, and Andi nodded. Abby wrapped her arms around her and hugged her unhurriedly, swaying back and forth.

Andi said, "You know what this makes me think of?"

"What?"

"Remember that really tall pine tree behind the house? I used to climb to the top. The trunk was so thin it could barely hold my weight, and the wind would gently sway me back and forth. I ran to that tree a lot when I was young. It was my comfort and refuge. I sobbed when Daddy had to have it taken down. I felt like I was losing my best friend. I loved the smell of the resin and needles."

"I remember you always loved trees."

"Yes, I did. They were my friends. In my early teen years, I spent a lot of time in the woods, and I talked to trees all the time. I even hugged them. I loved red maples and weeping willows and sycamores. When I left home, I told the trees goodbye and thanked them for loving me."

Abby knew it was a highly unusual moment for Andi to expose her vulnerability. She said nothing just nodded her understanding.

Andi smiled back and said, "Thanks for coming, sis."

Abby awakened after fitfully sleeping and much soul searching. *How many times must I turn this back over to You, Lord? Here, Andi's pregnant and doesn't want it. I'd take her baby in a heartbeat. And what about Isaac? I don't know what I did to turn him off, but frankly, I don't want to get involved with someone that moody anyway. What kind of life would that be?*

She was headed to Mr. Johnson's house. He was still in the hospital recovering from his infection at rehab, so she had rounded up some help to clean his house. She had purchased some cleaning supplies and was looking forward to it. She loved to clean when she was upset, so this was a great time to attack his dirt.

* * * * *

When she arrived, she was thrilled to see the outside transformation. The yard had been mowed, and the weeds trimmed. Trash had been piled at the end of the yard, ready to be hauled off. The house and porch had been power-washed. What a difference with the black-and-green mold gone. She stepped through the door, and two of her girlfriends were there. They were dragging his mattress down the hall.

"This thing needs a good airing," they said. She gave them a hand as they hauled it out on the porch to let the sunshine and fresh air revive it.

They each decided to take a room. Abby started in the kitchen.

"Oh my," she said as she stood in one place and slowly turned in a full circle. The kitchen cabinets were thick with grime. The refrigerator needed practically everything thrown away and scrubbed inside and out. She donned her apron and rubber gloves and went to work. She systematically threw out everything in the fridge and the cabinets that were bad. She ran sink after sink of hot soapy dishwater. She washed down all the cupboards inside and out, cleaned the stove, the refrigerator, the windows, and the counters. She scrubbed every inch of the kitchen table and all the chairs. She took down the curtains. They were so old they tore apart in her hands.

Abby's back was aching as she rode back down the mountain. It had taken five hours to clean the kitchen alone. She had a great team that had shown up. At the end of the day, Mr. Johnson's living room was clean, the carpet had been shampooed, and all the windows washed. They were coming back the following week to paint. When Mr. Johnson came back, he would be so pleased. He might not act like he was. She knew in his own special way he would be delighted. Abby realized she had grown to love him in spite of everything. She had visited him every single day in rehab. The last visit, she hugged him, and he awkwardly patted her back.

When she arrived home, there was a balloon tied to her front door with a card. She opened the card, and it read:

Abby,

Will you please meet me at Fresco's tonight at 6:00 p.m. I'd like to treat you to dinner so I can explain my behavior. If you choose not to come, I certainly understand, but I'm hoping you will. Thank you.

—Isaac

Abby's initial response was to toss the card in the trash. She didn't have enough energy. She slipped out of her dirty clothes and eased down into a bubble bath. As the hot water and aroma therapy soaked into her sore muscles, she began to pray. *Guide me, Lord. I don't want to get my heart broken. Isaac's treatment to me made me feel humiliated and rejected.*

Abby lay in the tub with her eyes closed, thinking about how a spirit of rejection had plagued her life for many years. *I'm so sick of this. I know it's just a spirit, and I have authority over it. Why can't I be done with this? Lord, help me. I've thought about this a million times, examined my heart, my past. I realize it started because Andi took up so much of Mom and Dad's time that I felt left out. Then, as a result, I became a people pleaser. I'm always afraid of disappointing someone. It's ridiculous. I can't bear anyone to be angry, and I'm constantly trying to be a peacemaker. It's a heavy load, and I know you are my burden bearer, Lord. Break this stronghold in my life, God. Help me to roll these cares over to You so I can be free.*

She stood at her closet door trying to decide whether to go in jeans or something a bit dressier. She chose her red sundress and sandals and was mad at herself for being excited to see him.

She opened the restaurant door, and there stood Isaac holding a bouquet of flowers. He walked toward her anxiously. He led her to a corner table and held her chair for her. Abby understood all too well as he told his story. It never occurred to her that Andi was once again dragging her into another difficult situation. Isaac was so sincere and humble that she assured him that all was forgiven.

"I know my sister has serious issues, Isaac. However, she is my sister. I pray for her all the time," said Abby.

Isaac said, "I'll pray for her too, Abby."

"Thank you Isaac, I appreciate it more than you know. And thank you for the flowers. They're beautiful."

* * * * *

Louise plotted and planned her strategy. She was cooking dinner when Jerry came in from the garden. She smiled at him when he walked into the kitchen.

Jerry felt intense relief. "Honey, I'm really proud of you for trying to put all of this behind you," he said as he washed his hands at the kitchen sink.

Louise just smiled and said, "I'm trying, dear." She had prepared his favorite meal: fried chicken. They ate in companionable silence.

Louise said, "Honey, I've been thinking. I'd like to visit Marge in Ohio for a few days. I haven't seen my sister in five years, and she's invited me to come."

Jerry said, "I think that's a great idea. Will you drive?"

Louise said, "I know I've always been silly about flying, but the drive is so long and exhausting. I think I'll go downtown tomorrow to the travel agency and check on pricing."

Jerry said, "Do you want me to go with you?"

She shook her head and said, "No, indeed, I'll be fine. Plus, I plan to buy Marge a gift while I'm in town."

Jerry was thankful as he went out to get the evening paper.

* * * * *

The travel agent was hopeful as she heard the beeper sound on the front door. She needed a sale. She got up and went around to the front. "Good morning. May I help you?"

"Yes," said Louise. She had dressed carefully and looked quite the lady. "I'd like to check on the price of a ticket. I'm going to see my sister, and this will be my first time to fly."

Jackie shook Louise's hand and said, "Certainly, come right this way. I'll be glad to check that for you." She sat in front of her computer and asked for her departure and return dates.

"I'd like to leave this Friday."

Jackie typed in the date. "What airport will you be flying into?"

"Washington Dulles," said Louise.

"And will you be returning from Virginia as well?"

"Yes, dear. I won't need a return ticket. My sister and I will drive back together."

Jackie's computer researched the best airline pricing, and in a very few minutes, Louise was booked for a direct flight to Virginia. Jackie handed her the receipt and assured her there was nothing to be afraid of.

* * * * *

Louise licked her lips nervously as her pulse increased to a rapid race. She was pulling out of Washington Dulles Airport in her rented white Dodge Intrepid as she wound her way into the flow of noon traffic. She had outlined the map and knew she was looking for Route 66 West. The road signs were clearly marked and easy to find.

She pulled into the Super 8 Motel and booked a room for the weekend. She swallowed a Xanax as she sat at the small desk in her room making a list. She reached over to her luggage and pulled out a small framed picture of Rebecca and sat it on her desk. She looked at it a long time as she began her list. *Mother's here, my darling, not to worry.*

An open bag lay on the floor with a coloring book and crayons, a teddy bear, a box of brown hair color, boy's jeans, a navy T-shirt, and a small baseball cap. She looked in the phone book for a hardware store and was soon on her way to pick up her needed supplies.

Louise meandered up and down the aisles when she spotted the bottle of chloroform. She purchased it along with bug spray, boric acid, and a large box of salt. Louise had her explanation ready that she was trying some homemade remedies her grandmother used to get rid of wasps and ants. But the checkout employee was a teen who couldn't care less. He had on baggy jeans way too big that slung down on his hips. His underwear was showing, and he had his wallet chained to his pants. That suited Louise just fine. She came in on a cane so she would appear helpless and harmless. She gave the kid a dollar to carry the bag to the car for her.

* * * * *

Mamaw Esther had awakened at precisely 3:00 a.m. for the third night in a row. She sat up and turned on the low bedside lamp. She knew when the Lord was calling her to intercede. She pulled the quilt up close and began to pray. She soon had to get up and walk. She pulled on her thick robe and slippers and walked down the hall to the living room. As she began to walk back and forth, the travail came. She fell to her knees praying from the depths of her soul. *Lord God, what is it?* Suddenly Andi's face came before her, and she stretched herself out on the living room floor, praying for her beloved granddaughter.

Papaw Thomas rose and dressed before dawn as he had for many years and went in search for hot coffee. As he walked down the hall, he knew something was amiss. He stepped in the living room, and there lay his precious bride asleep on the living-room floor. He felt no alarm as he had found her this way many a time over the years. He went to her and gently pulled her up.

"Come on, love, up you go."

Esther smiled at Thomas and said, "Good morning, darling. I'll have coffee ready in two minutes."

"No, Es, why don't you lie back down for a little while and warm up? I don't want you to get a cold."

"Fiddlesticks," replied Esther as she hobbled her stiff joints to the kitchen.

As they sat together in the breakfast nook sipping their coffee, Thomas said, "I had a dream last night."

Esther didn't ask any questions, just waited.

"In my dream, Andi was weeping."

Thomas took Esther's hand and gently squeezed it. They bowed their head as they prayed.

> *Lord, You love for us to put You in remembrance of Your Word. Matthew 18:19 says where two agree, so we're agreeing together, Lord. We lift up Andrea Marigold Alexander to you. Release Your angels, Lord God, to go and protect our precious girl. Soften her heart, Father. Draw her by Your Spirit, Lord. Make her hungry for You, Lord. Release Your righteous laborers in the field, Lord. We pray that You would put people in her path, whether she turns north, south, east, or west to point her toward the Cross and to show her Your love. Romans 2:4 says the goodness of God brings man to repentance. Accost her with Your love, Lord. We pray that the blinders would be removed from her eyes. We thwart and foil the plans of the enemy. We break the power of the enemy off her life. We claim her soul for the kingdom of God, and we pray for it to be a quick work in Jesus's name.*

* * * * *

Louise narrowed her eyes and smiled as she sipped her coffee at the five-and-dime counter. *Small towns are all alike*, she thought as she had hoodwinked her way into finding out where Isaac worked, where he lived, and where Becca's day-care center was located. She had slowly driven by the day care, parking back off the street. When playtime came, she scanned the children carefully with her binoculars until she spotted Rebecca. She could barely restrain herself from jumping out of the car to grab her granddaughter. "Mommy's here, baby. Don't worry, sweetheart, Mommy's here."

* * * * *

Isaac walked out of the bait shop when he ran into a patient from the clinic.

"Hi, Doc. Today's Tuesday. You're off on Tuesdays. You goin' fishin'?"

Isaac shook Donnie's hand as he smiled down at him. Donnie was an eight-year-old dwarf. His parents were both little people, but he had four older brothers that were average height, and the entire family were amazing musical prodigies. They could play every stringed instrument known to man.

"Yes, indeed, Donnie. I'm heading to the river."

"I know where there's good fishing, Doc," said Donnie excitedly.

Isaac waited, but Donnie just stood mute with shining eyes.

"Are you going to share your secret with your old friend?" asked Isaac, laughing.

Nodding, Donnie said in a whisper, "Go down to the landing and get yourself in a boat, then paddle down past the first bend, and there's a great big log over on the far left bank. Some nice fishin' in that dark hole, Doc Graham. That's our solemn secret, okay?" he said with a serious expression.

"Cross my heart," said Isaac as he crossed his heart and held up his right hand.

Isaac tried to make Abby put on a life jacket before she got in the boat, but she just laughed and said, "As low as this river is, even if I did fall in the water, it wouldn't be over my knees."

They had just pushed away from the bank when a huge black snake came skimming across the water. Isaac watched to see Abby's reaction, but it didn't faze her. She had packed a picnic basket and a blanket. Isaac slowly paddled as they relished the beautiful day. The trees were boasting in full fall colors, and they made a patchwork reflection on the water.

They were in no hurry. They took their time enjoying easy conversation, letting the boat drift. As they came around the first bend, sure enough, there was the log Donnie told him about. Isaac maneuvered the boat over and dropped the small anchor weight.

"Shall I bait your hook for you?" he asked.

"Don't insult me, mister. My Papaw taught me to fish when I was knee high to a duck, thank you very much," she said as she reached for the rod and reel. Isaac covertly watched her bait her hook and was definitely impressed. She cast into the exact right spot, and within two minutes, she had a bite. She expertly reeled in a blue gill the size of his hand.

"Nice job there, Abigail."

She cut her eyes at him and grunted.

"What?" he said. "Abigail is a nice name. What's your middle name?"

Abby ignored him.

"Is it Ann?" he asked.

"No."

"Is it Lynn?"

"No."

"Is it Marie?"

"No."

"What letter does it start with?"

Abby laughed and said, "You don't need to know."

"Why? Don't you like your middle name?" he asked.

"Not especially," she said.

"Is it a family name?"

"Yes."

"I'll tell you my middle name," he said innocently.

She said, "Thanks for offering. I'm not nosy…like some people."

"My middle name is your last name," he said, smiling.

She said, "Isaac Alexander Graham. Nice name, fits you." She cast again.

"Abigail something Alexander. Abigail Carol?"

"No," said Abby.

"Just tell me what letter it starts with," teased Isaac.

Abby rolled her eyes and said, "You know you're worse than a gnat. Okay, it starts with a *Z*."

Isaac laughed and said "*Z*? Are you serious?"

"Yes, she said, "and don't ask any more questions."

Isaac fished in silence for a while and softly said, "*Z*... Zulu?"

She gave him a stern look, and he said, "Okay, sorry." Suddenly his pole jerked, and he started reeling in. "Wow, looks like I've got a fighter." After what seemed an eternity, he finally landed a seven-pound catfish with the ugliest face she'd ever seen.

They had been on the river two hours with the fall sun warm overhead.

"I'm hungry. How about you?" asked Isaac as he pulled up the anchor. They rowed till they came to a nice landing area and spread out their blanket under a sycamore tree. Abby had packed egg salad sandwiches, carrot sticks, brownies, and a large thermos of lemonade.

"Would you like for me to give thanks?" asked Isaac.

Abby nodded as he took her hand, and he began to pray. "Lord, we want to thank You for this day to spend time together. We commit our fellowship to You and ask Your blessings on this food in Jesus's name."

Abby passed the food and realized she had forgotten to pack cups. She looked up as Isaac took a big drink from the thermos and handed it to her. The intimacy of sharing it made her blush. He enjoyed watching her turn blotchy red and openly stared at her smiling. Abby tried to ignore him. His watchful eye only made her more nervous.

After lunch, they sat propped against the tree trunk and enjoyed the shade and easy conversation. Abby was very comfortable with this man. They could sit quietly and just watch the river flow by. They shared their salvation stories and tidbits about their life.

"Did you feel called to be a nurse?" asked Isaac.

"Not really," said Abby. "I knew the work was solid and plentiful, and it pays well with good benefits."

"Did you have something else in mind?" asked Isaac.

Abby wasn't sure she was ready to be that vulnerable yet. She tended to guard her heart carefully. She had loved to write stories even from a young child and envisioned herself as a Christian author and itinerant speaker. She had written many poems that she hoped to get published, along with some short stories. She had a file of story starters. She had a vivid imagination and was always adding ideas to her file. She wanted her books to feed people spiritually and share God's love through her writings. Books would be her way to serve in ministry. Her aunt influenced her to go into nursing instead. Being a nurse had its ups and downs, but her heart's desire had always been in ministry.

"Sure, I wanted to join the circus," said Abby.

He looked at her and smiled. "Where do you see yourself in ten years?" Isaac asked.

Abby hated those kinds of questions. She'd never been the type to plan her life. She was impulsive and liked to fly by the seat of her pants.

"Oh, I don't know, Isaac. Serving the Lord with all my heart. Being obedient to His Word."

They were both leaning against the tree trunk. They sat quietly for a while enjoying each other's company. Abby found Isaac very attractive and had to work at not staring at him. Isaac leaned toward her, and she knew she was about to be kissed. As if in slow motion, he leaned down toward her, his eyes never leaving hers. He looked down at her mouth. Abby felt her pulse quicken as she shifted positions. She didn't kiss on a first date. He got the message and smiled sweetly at her. It melted Abby's heart. He leaned back against the tree and beckoned her to lean back beside him.

"Have you ever noticed how many shades of green there are?"

Abby cast her eyes downriver and joyed in the sights and sounds. The sounds were fluid and calming. The trees that lined the banks were peaceful and healing. They sat contentedly, not needing conversation.

"I haven't talked with you about the incident a few months ago. I didn't know if you were up to it."

She nodded but remained silent.

He reached for her hand. "It's okay. You don't have to talk about it."

"The incident"—she laughed—"you mean where I drowned, and you saved my life? It's not that I'm afraid or that it brings fear. It's just still so surreal. I'm so very grateful for you risking your life for me, Isaac."

"Shhh, no need to say that. I'm glad you decided to come back to the river. I think it's very healthy."

Abby said, "All my life, I've found solace at this river. It's such a part of me. It's like an old friend. When I look back at my life, every time I had a major decision or crisis, I always went to the river to pray and get centered. I have a lot of great childhood memories here too. My parents loved to camp, and they took Andi and me several times a year. We'd pitch a tent and fish and cook over an open fire. We took a bath in the river and splashed and swam. When it was really scorching hot, Mom and Dad would set their lawn chairs right in the water while we played. And my grandparents' farm had a tributary that ran into the river. It was a great creek that my Papaw taught us to swim in and fish.

"That particular day, I wanted to take some photos of the river. Remember that big storm we had? It rained heavily for three straight days and flooded the area. The river had barely gone back into its banks, and I wanted to get some shots. I love photography, and I have an interesting collection of the valley. As I was walking the bank that dog came running toward the water and ran into me. It all happened so fast it still seems like a dream. I was terrified. Then again, it was over before I had time to think about it. The water was so swift that I was tossed around like a rag doll. I'm so thankful I had presence of mind to grab that branch."

"Did you have an after-life experience, Abby?"

She nodded without looking at him.

"Would you like to share it with me? It's okay if you don't want to." Isaac studied her profile as she sat staring at the river.

She stood and leaned against the tree. She said, "I don't really know what to say." She sat pensively, looking downstream. "Heaven is real, Isaac. I mean, I know we all know it is real. I saw just a glimpse, and there are just no adequate words to describe it. It's beyond beautiful. It's amazing. It's complete. I'm finding it difficult to describe what I saw and felt. In heaven, you have more senses than the five we have here. Everything is so alive, vibrant, colorful and...like it's pulsating with love and worship. I saw colors we don't have here."

"What kind?"

"I don't know."

"Can't you describe it?"

"No, I can't. It's unlike anything here, nothing compares, nothing."

"Is it like blue or gold?"

"No, it's not. I'm sorry. I've tried to analyze what I saw. It's not varying shades or hues of anything here. Everything there is just more...better, pure and alive and untainted. I saw Jesus face-to-face."

"Wow. Can you describe what He looked like?"

"The only thing I really remember were His eyes. His eyes were liquid love."

"Were they brown?"

"No, I don't think so."

"Were they green or blue?"

"I'm not sure. They were fathomless. Like the depths of the sea and so filled with love. I wanted to be with Him so much, and He wanted to be with me too. It just wasn't my time."

"Did you see anything else?"

Abby's eyes filled with tears as she described her loved ones looking over the portal.

"You should give a testimony about this, Abby."

"I don't want to be selfish, Isaac, but I feel inadequate talking about this. I wouldn't know how to answer people's questions."

"It would give people hope and peace."

Abby nodded and said, "I'll think about it."

"Did it frighten you?"

"No, not at all. I yearned to be with Him. I've thought about it a lot, and I guess I feel overwhelmed that the Lord sent me back. What am I supposed to do with my life? I'm just an ordinary person, Isaac. I can't imagine doing mighty exploits for God. I barely have enough nerve to talk to you. I'm just a home health nurse."

She closed her eyes. "Jesus told me my destiny here on earth wasn't finished yet, and it's made me feel overwhelmed. How can I possibly make a difference? I'm just one person in a small town in the valley. I'm nothing special."

Isaac turned to her and took both of her hands. As he got ready to speak, she said, "Please, Isaac, can we change the subject? I'm extremely uncomfortable right now. I know you want to encourage me, and I truly appreciate that. I promise to give you an opportunity to share your heart, but just for today, can we just keep it light?"

Isaac nodded and patted the quilt for her to sit back down.

After sitting contentedly quiet for a few minutes, Isaac said, "I was at church a few weeks ago when you sang 'We Shall Behold Him.'"

She sat up and turned around to look at him. She blushed up to the roots of her hair. Isaac chuckled and said, "Please don't be embarrassed. It was wonderful. That was my first Sunday in the valley. I was looking for a church for me and Becca, and I sure liked what I found. When did you learn sign language?"

"My dad is deaf. So we learned it from babies."

"Was he born deaf?"

"No. Actually, he lost his hearing when he was in the army. He was standing behind a large piece of artillery. When it went off, he and all the men standing with them were knocked unconscious by the sound. It blew out their eardrums."

"Oh wow. Did it make all of them deaf?"

"I'm not sure. I know they all had hearing defects, but my dad lost all of his hearing. He was twenty-one at the time. He went to sign-language school. When he met my mom, she went to classes, and they ended up getting married."

"Is your sister as fluent as you are?"

"Yes, she is."

"That's so incredible."

Abby smiled. "Yes, I guess it is. We take it for granted since it's all we've ever known."

"Do you ever interpret anywhere else?"

"Yes, Andi and I have taught classes at the community center, and my whole family has been called on to help in emergencies at the hospital or other places where deaf people need help."

"Have you ever considered doing it professionally, like a business?"

"When I finished high school, I considered going to school to be a certified ASL interpreter and instructor, mostly to interpret at ministerial events but on a bigger scale."

"You mean like Billy Graham concerts?"

"Yes, exactly."

"Why didn't you?"

Abby looked away and shrugged. Isaac let it drop. They sat quietly for a while. They were both comfortable in each other's presence, not needing to fill the quiet with idle chatting.

"Can you play an instrument?" asked Isaac.

"A little, but it's been a while. Andi and I were both in the high school marching band. Andi played the clarinet when she wasn't playing hooky, and I played the flute," said Abby.

"Were you any good?" asked Isaac.

Abby laughed and said "I was good for a kid. I had first chair in the band. Learning to play came easily for me."

"Do you still play?" asked Isaac.

"No, I haven't played for several years," said Abby. "How about you? Are you musical?" she asked.

"I sing and play the guitar," he replied.

"Are you good?" she asked.

He said, "Well, yes, actually, I am, but I give God the glory."

"Would you play and sing for me sometime?" asked Abby.

He grinned mischievously and said, "Sure. I will if you tell me your middle name."

Abby hopped up and said, "You're impossible. No one will ever know my middle name."

"Not even your husband?" he said warmly.

"That's the only exception." She knew she was going to blush again, so she shoved him sideways and said, "Come on, we'd better head back."

Suddenly Isaac felt troubled in his spirit. He looked at his watch and stared across the river.

Abby said, "Is anything wrong?"

"Well, I know this might sound crazy, but suddenly I feel really anxious about Becca," he answered.

"Where is she today?" asked Abby.

He answered, "She's at Living Water Daycare. I'm sure she's fine. I don't know why I feel like this all of a sudden."

"We're finished here," said Abby, gathering up the lunch basket. "Would you like to check on her?"

Isaac said, "I'm sorry, Abby."

Abby said, "Don't be silly, let's go."

As they got ready to climb into the boat, Isaac's heart started racing, and he started to sweat. "Abby, I don't know what's going on, but I feel crazy with fear. Let's pray."

Isaac hit his knees and started fervently praying out loud. Abby was also a strong Christian, but his intensity made her feel uncomfortable. He dropped down on his face on the ground and started shouting his prayer. Abby started praying too as the intercession fell on her as well.

"I plead the blood of Jesus!" Isaac was shouting.

They quickly jumped in the boat and rowed back to the landing.

* * * * *

Louise had brought a puppy to the church playground. She was walking the puppy on a leash very close to the edge of the playground where Becca was playing. Louise was frantic to get her hands on Becca. She had waited for the right timing. She had wanted to leave on Monday, but she had found out Isaac's day off was Tuesday and had to wait an extra day before her plans finally came together.

When Louise saw that the teacher had gone to the other side of the play area to attend to a crying child, Louise said, "Hi, Rebecca."

Becca looked up and said, "Do you know me?"

Louise said, "Of course, I do, sweetheart." Louise had on a wig, a scarf, and sunglasses. She had to disguise herself so no one could identify her. "I'm a friend of your daddy's."

"Oh," said Becca, but she hung back. Isaac had taught her well all of her life not to talk to strangers.

Louise said, "Would you like to see my puppy?" The puppy was a butterball yellow Lab with a wagging tail. Louise edged closer, and Becca eased her hand out to touch the puppy's head.

"He's so sweet," said Becca.

"Yes, he is, and you know what, sweetheart? I bought him just for you."

"You did? For me, a puppy? Oh, thank you."

Louise said sweetly, "You're welcome, darling. Why don't we go surprise your daddy right now?"

"Okay," said Becca trustingly.

Louise glanced up and saw the teacher was still attending to the scraped knee when she calmly took Becca's hand and walked to the wooded area.

"Where are we going?" asked Becca. She suddenly felt afraid that she would be punished for walking away with a stranger. She tried to pull back, but Louise walked a little faster and said reassuringly, "I'm parked right over here, sweetie. We're going to see your daddy and show him your new puppy. Daddy said I could come and surprise you."

"He did? Oh, okay," said Becca with relief as she skipped to the car.

Louise had stopped at Walmart to buy a car seat. She buckled her in and laid the puppy on the seat beside her.

She pulled into the Super 8 motel and turned off the engine. "We'll just stop in here for a minute to get my bag, then we'll go straight home to see Daddy."

* * * * *

Isaac and Abby jumped into Isaac's SUV as Isaac dialed the day care from his cell. He spoke into the phone, "She's out on the playground?" He desperately wanted to believe it, but he still felt frantic. "Could you just go check to be sure?" He was driving fast when she came back on the line. "Call the police, I'm on my way. She's gone, Abby. She was on the playground, and she's disappeared. Nobody saw anything. Jesus, Jesus, help me, dear God."

Abby started praying out loud as the speedometer read ninety miles per hour.

Abby's parents had decided to splurge and eat out. Mark and Carolyn were on their way to the steakhouse when they saw Isaac's black Ford Excursion fly by. Carolyn craned her neck back and caught a glimpse of her daughter Abby in the passenger seat. "Turn around quick. Something's wrong," she signed to mark. Mark made a quick U-turn and hurried to catch up with the SUV.

"I hope we don't get a ticket," signed Carolyn.

"At this point, I don't care," Mark quickly signed back. He floored it and ran a red light. He could barely see the taillights in front of him, but he was not going to let them get away from him. They were both praying as he realized they headed for Living Water Church.

Isaac threw the truck in park and took off running. Police cars were everywhere. Abby turned the key off and burst into tears as her mom and dad pulled in. She ran to them as they folded her in their arms. "Honey, what happened?" asked her mom.

"Becca's disappeared off the school grounds," she said.

Her dad put his arm around her as they walked toward the school. The teacher's face was red and swollen where she had been crying.

"She was right there, playing. Little Sam fell and scraped his knee, and I was putting a Band-Aid on him on the picnic table. She wasn't fifty feet from me. I didn't hear a thing. I didn't see anything out of the ordinary."

Isaac had to control himself from screaming. He felt nauseated and paced like a caged lion.

* * * * *

Jerry was worried. Louise said she was coming home Monday night, and it was Tuesday morning. He decided to call the airline to make sure it hadn't been delayed. The operator came on with, "I'm sorry, sir, we have no Louise James booked on a flight from Ohio." Jerry hung up, feeling dread. "Louise, what have you done?" He felt sick with worry. He knew she had been under severe anxiety, but she had seemed to be so much better. *It was all an act*, he thought. He called the travel agency, and they confirmed she had booked a one-way flight to Virginia.

Jerry didn't know what to do. He felt helpless so far away. He had to warn Isaac. He dialed his home number and got a recording. He wasn't sure what to say on a message, so he hung up. He dialed his cell number, and Isaac answered on the first ring.

"Isaac, this is Jerry. Louise told me she was going to Ohio to visit Marge and was supposed return last evening, but she's not here. I called the airline, and she flew to Virginia. I think I need to warn you, Isaac. She may try to find Becca."

"She kidnapped Becca!" Isaac shouted into the phone. "Where is she, Jerry? For the love of God, where is she!" he yelled like a crazy man into the phone.

Jerry said, "I don't know, Isaac. I'm sorry, son, I just don't know."

Isaac shoved the phone to the police, grabbed the trash can, and vomited.

* * * * *

Becca was playing with the puppy on the bed as Louise sat beside her, smiling. "Mommy's so, so glad to see you, darling."

Becca looked up at her, alarmed, and said, "My mommy's an angel. She's in heaven."

Louise reached over and picked her and hugged her tightly.

Becca strained against her, crying, "I want Daddy."

"Here, I bought some toys for you to play with. I just have a few things to do, and we'll go see Daddy." She handed the bear and other toys to Becca. Becca wouldn't play with them. She sat on the floor, eyeing Louise. Louise took off her wig and glasses and scarf.

"Nana?" said Becca.

Louise stepped into the bathroom and soaked the washcloth with chloroform. "Come here, sweetie, let's get your hands and face washed, and we'll go to Daddy right now."

Becca warily came to the bathroom as Louise grabbed her and covered her mouth and nose with the washcloth. Becca fought hard, but Louise had her in a vise grip. It took about thirty seconds for her to collapse. Louise stripped off her clothes and soaked her blonde hair with the hair dye. She grabbed the boy clothes and hurriedly dressed her. She rinsed her hair and hacked it short. She threw the hair in the wastebasket and pulled the baseball cap down over her head. She gathered up everything in the room except the dog and hauled it to the trunk. Then she ran back and carried Becca to the car. She left the puppy whining in the motel room as she sped out of the parking lot.

The police had put an all-points bulletin out for her. All the crossroads and interstates were having road checks. Becca's name and description had already been posted on the Amber alert at all the airports, bus terminals, and truck stops.

The church prayer chain had been alerted to pray for Becca. Louise had planned to drive about six hours then stop for the night. She couldn't wait to get her baby home where she belonged. She was headed for the interstate when she saw a long line of traffic. Panic seized her as she saw the flashing lights. There was no way to turn around. She rolled her window down as the officer asked for license and registration. He eyed the sleeping four-year-old in the back. She told the officer her purse had been stolen at the last restaurant. The officer said, "Step out of the car please."

She said in a strained voice, "Oh no, please, I can't leave my little girl—I mean, my grandson."

He opened her door and said in a firm voice, "Step out of the car, ma'am, now!"

She sat still and stared straight ahead.

"I'm going to ask you once more, ma'am. Step out of the vehicle." He reached for her arm.

She jerked away from him, stomping the accelerator. She floored it and broke through the roadblock. The officer quickly called for backup and took off after her. "She has the child in the backseat," he spoke over the radio. He continued speaking, "There's no way the child could have slept through that. She must be drugged. Be careful, don't make her drive too fast. We need to rescue the child." The police radioed ahead, and spike mats were laid down in the highway. Louise grabbed the wheel as her tires blew. Louise was screaming as the car careened wildly from side to side. The car flipped twice and landed on its top, sliding on the pavement. Sparks were flying as the car slid to a stop. The police car squealed to a stop and jumped out, aiming his pistol at the driver. He eased over to the driver's side and saw blood pouring from Louise's ear. He felt her pulse. She was alive but barely. The little girl was still buckled in upside down. He unbuckled and carried her limp body back to his car.

"I have the child. She appears unharmed, but we need a chopper over here fast. The driver's in bad shape," he spoke to the dispatcher.

A medical helicopter landed, and medics rushed over to the woman and child.

"They have Becca. They're flying her to the hospital," the officer told Isaac.

Isaac grabbed Abby's hand as they ran for his truck. The sheriff's office gave him a fast escort to the hospital. They pulled into the parking lot just as the helicopter was touching down on the landing pad. Isaac jumped the concrete wall and sprinted for his daughter. He felt her pulse. Rage ripped through him as he jerked off her baseball cap and saw her chopped hair that had been dyed brown. He looked at the boy's clothes and ran with her in his arms into the ER. She awakened to him bending over her.

"Daddy, my head hurts."

"It's okay, sweetie."

"Where's my puppy?" she asked as she drifted back out.

Two hours later, Isaac raked his hand through his hair exhausted from adrenaline rushing through his body. He laid his head on the side of the bed, crying with gratitude that she was safe.

Louise was in critical condition. Abby checked on her. and the head nurse said she had a critical head injury and bleeding in her brain. She also had multiple broken bones. Her husband had been called, and he was flying in on the next flight.

Abby found Isaac still sitting in the chair beside Becca's bed. He looked completely exhausted. Abby slowly approached. "Want some company?" she said softly. "Or would you rather be alone?"

He looked weary and whispered, "Please join me." He pulled a chair beside him, and she sat down.

Isaac said, "The doctor said she's fine. It was chloroform, and thank God not a lethal dose. He gave her a clean bill of health. She wasn't hurt at all. Her pediatrician gave her a light sedative and said she would stay overnight for observation and be ready to go home in the morning."

They were silent for a few minutes when Abby said, "I checked on Louise." She felt him stiffen. "They don't think she'll make it."

Isaac never flinched but said, "Good, that'll keep me from going to prison for murder."

Abby understood that he was emotional, but she silently prayed for him.

"Why don't you go home and rest, Isaac? Get a hot shower and a change of clothes before you settle in to stay the night. I'll be glad to stay right here. I'll never leave her side," Abby offered.

"No, but thanks for the offer. I can't leave my baby." He reached over to Becca and pushed her bangs off her forehead. He ran his hand through her chopped hair. It had streaks of blonde still showing. Her hair was so short it had been cut all the way to the scalp on the sides.

Abby said, "I think I'll head home. I'll talk to you later, okay? If you need me, call me."

He stood up and put his arms around her. He gave her a long hug and said, "Thank you, Abby. I loved our time together today."

"Me too," said Abby.

Mark and Carolyn were waiting in the lobby as Abby walked out.

"Oh gosh, Mom, Dad, I'm so sorry, you've been waiting all this time," Abby signed to them.

"Nonsense," her mother signed back. "How is Becca?"

Abby answered wearily, "Thank God, she's unharmed. Evidently, his mother-in-law had a nervous breakdown and kidnapped her. She's in critical condition from the accident. She has a broken neck and broken back and a critical brain bleed."

Carolyn said, "We'll pray for her, honey. Are you okay, sweetheart?"

"Yes, I'm fine, just drained," said Abby.

"Can we do anything for you? Let us get you some dinner."

"Oh no, thank you so much. I just want to go home. I'm going to take a hot bath and get to bed early," replied Abby.

Her mom hugged her tight and kissed her goodbye.

Her dad hugged her too, signing, "You know where we are if you need us, babe."

Abby felt loved as she walked out to the parking lot. "Mom," she called.

Carolyn tapped Mark to turn around.

Abby signed, "I forgot my car's not here."

He smiled and signed, "We'll run you home. Hop in."

* * * * *

Mr. Johnson was being released to go home. As the nurses were reading the bulletin board for their daily assignments, they prepared to draw straws again. This time, it was for who would have the privilege of tending Mr. Johnson.

Abby said, "Now wait just a minute. I am absolutely not drawing for this. I am going, and that's the end of it."

"No, Abby, fair is fair. We've always drawn straws, and it's not stopping now," said Jean.

Abby was fuming, but she had resolved she would go to see him after work if she had to. She couldn't wait to see his face when he saw the transformation of his home.

"You go first, Abby," said Jean.

Abby glared at the nurses as she jerked out a straw. It was the short one. She laughed and said, "Oh, I'm so glad."

All the nurses burst out laughing as they each drew a straw. They were all short. She hugged each one. They made sure she drew the short straw.

They all said, "After all you've done for him. You deserve it."

Abby packed her gear and excitedly drove out of the parking lot. She had two other stops to make before heading up the mountain. She had been on the cell phone and arranged to follow the ambulance. As they carried Mr. Johnson toward his porch, his raised up on one elbow and said, "Wait a minute here. What's this I see?"

All the hospital staff had gotten in on the project. Azalea bushes had been planted against the front porch. There was a porch swing, a rocker, and a hummingbird feeder. The house was so clean it was shining like a new penny. The yard was immaculate.

"I think y'all done brung ole Johnson to the wrong house," said Mr. Johnson.

They opened the door and stopped to let him look around. The carpet had been pulled out, and hardwood floors had been refinished and buffed to a shine. There was a new big oval braided rug on the floor. His dilapidated recliner had been replaced with a new one. He had a new digital TV. The old one with rabbit ears had found its way to the dump. The small kitchen was spotless. New yellow-and-brown plaid curtains hung at the windows. The nurses had gone wild with their generosity. The kitchen had been painted a pale yellow. There were new glasses and a new set of Corell plates for four. They bought a new coffeemaker and four new mugs. He had boiled his coffee before. The bathroom had been practically gutted. The men had ripped out the tub and put in a big shower that he could roll his wheelchair into. The bathroom was painted fresh and clean.

Mr. Johnson was speechless. He lay back down, drained from excitement.

"Come on, sweet pea," said the squad nurse. "Let's get you comfortable."

They pulled down the covers of his new adjustable bed, and the driver laid him down as gentle as a baby. They pushed a button and raised his head. The room was every shade of blue imaginable. The walls were a soft gray blue, and his bedspread and curtains and rug were varying shades of blue plaid. Tears trickled down his cheeks as he looked at the wall facing him. Someone had painted on the wall in beautiful script: "Jesus, Rose of Sharon, Lily of the Valley, Lion of the Tribe of Judah, Chief Cornerstone, Bright Morning Star, I Am,

Alpha and Omega, the Way, the Truth and the Life, King of Kings, Lord of Lord, True Vine, Bread of Life." On and on it read.

The ambulance drivers left as Abby walked over to the bed. She took his vitals and marked them on her chart. She thought he had dozed off when he reached over for her hand. She bent down and kissed his forehead.

"I thanks you, Miss Abby. Truly from my heart, I thanks you."

She wrapped her arms around him for a big hug.

Abby tucked him in and pulled his curtains.

"Your phone's right here, and we have a nurse staying nights until you recover enough to get around on your own."

Jeb Johnson was so tired he didn't even argue. He opened his eyes and looked up to see a few glow-in-the-dark stars on his ceiling. He was so touched that he prayed for the first time in a very long time. He began to recite out loud, "The Lord is my shepherd, I shall not want. He maketh me to lie down in green pastures, He leadeth me beside the still waters. He restoreth my soul: He leadeth me in the paths of righteousness for His name's sake. Yea, though I walk through the valley of the shadow of death, I will fear no evil: for Thou art with me. Thy rod and Thy staff, they comfort me. Thou preparest a table before me in the presence of mine enemies. Thou anointest my head with oil, my cup runneth over. Surely goodness and mercy shall follow me all the days of my life, and I will dwell in the house of the Lord forever."

* * * * *

Dot and Eddie Kingsley were great neighbors for Isaac. They minded their own business but were there if you needed them. The first week after Isaac moved in, Dot had brought a coconut cake with a warm greeting of "Welcome to the Neighborhood," and Eddie had brought tomatoes, squash, and zucchini from his garden. Isaac was so thankful Becca was a good eater. So many children in his practice only ate fast food. He had never started Becca on that fare, and as a result, she had developed a taste for real food. She loved vegetables. At the going-away party the church had for him in Kentucky, the church had had a big barbecue. Becca had shocked everyone when she ate bratwurst and sauerkraut.

Dot was a little nosy, but Isaac tolerated it to not make trouble, but trouble came in the form of Dot's granddaughter. Dot was trying to matchmake. She had invited Isaac for dinner one evening when she knew Becca was at a sleepover. When he arrived, there were four places set at the table.

Brenda came down the stairs in a startling green dress just as Dot said, "Isaac, I want you to meet our granddaughter. Brenda, this is our new neighbor, Isaac Graham—Dr. Isaac Graham. He's a widower and as nice as he can be. Isaac, this is Brenda Andrews. She's single, never married, a good Christian girl, thirty-two years old, and is a great little cook and homemaker. We thought you two would hit it off fine."

Isaac had to control himself not to roll his eyes and walk out. He felt sorry for Brenda as he turned to greet her, assuming she'd be as embarrassed as he was. But no—she stood grinning like a Cheshire cat.

They sat down to a dinner of meat loaf and fresh vegetables from the garden. After blessing the food, Dot said, "Isaac, do you like children? Well, of course, you do, silly me. You have a four-year-old, don't you? Bless her little heart. She needs a mother."

On and on, she peppered him with pointed questions until the whole pitiful affair struck him funny. It was all Isaac could do not to laugh. He thought of hilarious answers in his mind to her ridiculous questions. But of course, he was too polite to answer disrespectfully. After dinner, Isaac was hoping to be able to extract himself from their grip, but Dot proudly handed him an envelope. It was two movie tickets, and she said, "We wanted to treat you young people to a movie show. If you leave right now, you should get there just in time for a box of popcorn before the movie starts."

Brenda jumped up and said, "Oh, how lovely, Aunt Dot. Thank you. I'll just run up and grab my sweater."

Isaac was disgusted but knew it was pointless to say anything that would make a difference, and he didn't want to make a scene. He hated manipulation with a passion. As they stood in line for the tickets, Brenda slipped her arm through his. Isaac was surprised at how forward she was. He kept repositioning himself to get out of her embrace.

Abby was driving home after a long day of work. Her shoulder blades were burning with fatigue. Suddenly she caught sight of Isaac and a young woman clinging to his arm in line for the movie. Abby felt jealousy course through her.

As soon as the credits rolled, Isaac got up to leave. Brenda hinted that she would like to stop for a soda, but he said he was on call and had to be up early the next morning. He walked into his house, thankful to have gotten out alive. He sat down in his recliner with the lights out and looked down over the valley out the living-room window. He started praying at how to handle these situations in the future without causing offense to his neighbors. He would, in fact, like to meet someone special. Immediately, Abby's lovely face came to mind.

* * * * *

Andi awakened to the sound of birds chirping loudly. She glared at the clock: 5:40 a.m. She crawled out of bed and headed for the bathroom. She looked at herself in the mirror. She literally saw the blood drain out of her face as her stomach lurched and heaved. Would this infernal nausea ever stop? She was still disgusted with herself as she thought of how the hospital chaplain had talked her into canceling her abortion.

"It's a life," he said. "God has a plan."

She should have gone in drunk, and she wouldn't have had to listen to his mealymouthed sermon. Now she was three months along and miserable. She was on thin ice at work, having missed so much time from being sick. Being in a loud smoke-filled bar was definitely not jiving with her morning sickness. *Morning? I should be so lucky. I'm sick as a dog 24-7*, she thought. She has lost eight pounds and could only hold down saltines and ginger ale. She had been given information about a woman who lived down by the docks that knew about herbs and potions, and for a price, she could help her out. She had no qualms about contacting her. She had hardened her heart and was going to find her that very night.

Andi's skin crawled as she walked down the dark alley. It was littered with broken glass and trash, and graffiti scrawled along the walls. She found the place. It looked more like a run-down hovel than a home. There was a small shaft of light coming from under the door. Andi nervously walked up to the door and tapped. A woman that looked like a gypsy opened the door. Andi had to control herself not to run. She stated her business, and the woman opened the door wide enough for her to enter. The house was dark other than candles burning all over the place. The woman had on a long printed skirt and had unkempt shoulder-length gray hair. They sat at a table that had seen better days while Andi explained that she was thirteen weeks pregnant and wanted to abort.

The woman looked her in the eyes with a long searching stare as she laid out a row of tarot cards then reached for her hand. Andi flinched but didn't pull her hand back. The woman turned her hand over and stared at her palm.

After a few moments, she jumped up. "You have to leave," she said nervously. Andi stared at her, and the woman said it again with fear in her voice, "I can't help you."

Andi said, "What? Why? What's wrong?"

The woman walked toward the door and said, "Your covering is too strong for me. Get out." She literally shoved her out the door and slammed it.

"Covering?" said Andi. "What in the world is she talking about?"

Andi started back toward her car when she smelled cigarette smoke and heard shuffling of feet. She started walking fast when a man called out, "Well, well, well, what do we have here? Hey, pretty thing, what's your hurry?"

A strong hand grabbed her arm in a vise-like grip, squeezing her wrist. She cried out in pain. The man's eyes were pure evil. She quickly looked away as fear and panic rose like bile in her throat. Behind him, two enormous men were running toward her. Adrenaline coursed through her. Perspiration trickled down her neck, and she knew she was going to vomit. The evil man grabbed a fistful of hair, jerking her head back.

"How about a kiss?"

His putrid breath made her gag. The searing pain in her scalp nearly made her pass out. She thought her neck would snap if he forced her head back another fraction of an inch. Suddenly he released her with such force she staggered backward. The two gigantic men grabbed him with their massive arms, jerking him off the ground. They were at least two feet taller than him. She trembled looking at them. They looked so powerful. Andi broke into a dead run. Her lungs were burning, and her side ached. She could see her car, and it renewed her strength to keep running. As she unlocked the door, she looked back. The tall men were gone, but the man that had grabbed her was writhing on the ground. She started the car and took off, spinning gravel.

* * * * *

Laurie was sipping hot tea when Dale walked into the kitchen. He sat his cereal bowl on the table and started pouring his Cheerios.

"What's wrong, babe?"

She looked up at him with unshed tears in her eyes. "I'm not pregnant," she whispered.

"Oh, honey." He opened his arms, and she got up and walked over to him. She sat on his lap, and he let her cry into his chest. "You can't go on like this. Let's just accept the fact that we're not going to have any children of our own."

Laurie couldn't answer and just cried on his shoulder.

"What about adoption, Laurie? I'll tell you what, why don't I make an appointment for us to talk to Pastor Kobe? I know he's networked other families and helped them adopt. Let's just talk to him."

Laurie nodded and sighed as she laid her head on his shoulder.

Laurie sat in the guest bedroom, imagining how she would decorate it for a nursery. *Lord*, she prayed, *I know I have to get to the point where if I never have child, I have to be okay with it. But I'm not okay.*

I'm consumed with it, and I don't know how to control myself. Please help me. She imagined if she had a baby boy, she would paint the room pastel blue with puffy clouds on the ceiling. She would have shelving on the walls to hold a baseball, glove, and bat, a big jar of marbles, and a train set. She would have a toy airplane suspended from the ceiling with a long ribbon tail that would curve across the ceiling. If she had a baby girl, she would have pale-pink walls with framed pictures of hot-pink Gerber daisies. She would have a canopy bed with a quilted pink-and-green striped coverlet and a rocker to rock her baby. She would have a low table with a tea set and would place her old doll cradle in the corner with lots of baby dolls and stuffed animals. The women's ministry at church would throw her a shower, and her grandmother would sew a quilt for her like she had done for so many others.

* * * * *

Mazie McIntyre was a resident at Morning Side Assisted Living Facility. Nearly all of her family was gone, all except one great-niece, Victoria Ambrose. She stood with her eyes blazing and her hands on her hips. She was quite the sight in her fuchsia velour sweatsuit and her multiple pink beads around her neck. She was highly insulted when the head nurse asked her if she had taken the extension phone again. The nurse smiled as she heard the phone ringing from the confines of Miss Mazie's pocketbook on her arm. "Upon my honor, I did not steal your telephone." Brenda, the nurse, had too much heart to embarrass her by opening her purse and taking it out. She would nab it from her during her nap time.

They had painted her room light pink. She had dozens and dozens of framed paintings of pink roses she had painted herself. Her signature color was definitely pink. She had a pink lampshade, a pink quilt on her bed, and lots of pink jewelry. She had pink slippers, a pink robe, and a pink pocketbook. Mazie was not quite five feet tall and weighed about eighty-seven pounds. She had pink glasses and wore her hair in a beehive on top of her head. It was dyed dark brown, and she liberally wore pink everything from clothing to jewelry to blush. She was ninety-three years old and still as spry as a spring chicken. They had to watch her like a hawk. She could slip out the door before anyone would notice. The last time she had taken off, they had to call the police for a search. They found Miss Mazie walking down the highway, struggling with a heavy trash bag over her shoulder. The trash bag had shoes, the facility's telephone, silverware, a vase, a framed photograph, and a handful of ink pens and her pink quilt. When the officer pulled up beside her and asked if she was Mazie Groves, she replied, "Yes, I am, sweetheart." She didn't know where she was going or where she lived. She happily got in with him and told him some fascinating stories from her childhood. The officer enjoyed her so much that he came in with her and continued chatting awhile. They had tried putting monitors on her, beepers, ankle bracelets that would go off, but she was just like Houdini and always wiggled out of them. Fortunately, she was everyone's favorite, which was a blessing because she was a lot of trouble at times.

About the time you could get really aggravated with her, she would begin to sing and yodel, or tap dance, or get up to preach. And could she ever preach a sermon. She preached hellfire and damnation and made sure everyone prayed the sinner's prayer. You'd better pray with her, or she'd have a fit. It was not uncommon to hear her walking the halls at night praying for the nations. And she loved to cover everyone up to their neck with a warm blanket. Poor Mr. Tapscott was so hot-natured but would patiently allow her to tuck him in up to his chin; then he'd kick all the covers back off when she'd go out.

Funny thing about Miss Mazie: when she was praying, her prayers seemed to supersede her dementia. All the staff at one time or another had asked her to pray for them. When she prayed, things happened.

* * * * *

Jerry knocked on Isaac's door at the clinic.

"Come in," called Isaac.

Jerry eased the door open and said, "Can I talk to you, Isaac?"

Isaac immediately came to his feet.

"Isaac, I have no words to say how truly sorry I am that Louise caused you so much pain and fear. I praise God that Becca wasn't hurt. Louise is not expected to live through the week. I have to have her flown back for the funeral, and I have a lot of arrangements to make. I had to get away from the hospital for a while to clear my head. I just wanted to come and shake your hand. You were a wonderful husband to Rebecca and are a wonderful father to my granddaughter. When all this is said and done, I hope you will consider letting me see her from time to time. I won't take her away, but I hope you'll let me be a small part of her life. She's the only family I'll have left."

Isaac had resolved to write them out of his life, but looking at Jerry, his resolve melted. He hugged Jerry and said, "I would never rob my daughter from her heritage of having you as a grandfather. You're a good man. I'm sorry about Louise. Truly, I am. Unresolved grief and unforgiveness can drive a person to do horrible things. I forgive her, Jerry."

Jerry said, "Isaac, I know this is asking a lot, but would you consider coming to the hospital and telling her that. I know she's in a coma, but I believe she can hear. You telling her that might allow her to die in peace."

Isaac dreaded even the thought, but he heard himself agree to come that day when he got off work. After Jerry left, he sat staring into space. *You sneaked that one in on me, didn't You, Lord?* The corners of his mouth turned up as he reflected on the goodness and mercy of God.

* * * * *

Isaac looked down at Louise's swollen bandaged face and truly felt pity and compassion. He chose to remember her great cooking and warm hospitality she had shown him and Rebecca. The only sounds were the beeping of the hospital monitors hooked up to her battered body. Jerry stood at the foot of the bed as Isaac gently lifted Louise's hand. "Louise," he said softly, "it's Isaac. Little Becca is safe and unharmed. And I forgive you. All is well, Louise. Be at peace."

There was no sign of outward change. Jerry walked over and squeezed Isaac's shoulder. "Thank you, son. This means more to me than you'll ever know."

Isaac bent down and kissed Louise's forehead.

Isaac walked out of the hospital into the crisp fall air. It was a star-spangled night with a bright moon. He leaned against his truck as he breathed in the fragrance of peace. As he looked at the stars, he was overwhelmed that these were the same stars Abraham, Moses, and Peter had looked at. With a peaceful heart, he started for home.

* * * * *

Andi was grateful to no longer be nauseous. She was six and a half months along and quite large. She had lost her job at the bar and had taken a job waitressing. She was almost making enough tips to cover rent. The fact that she paid close to the full amount each month and made up the rest during the month kept her landlord from evicting her. She wasn't sure if she made such good tips because she was a good waitress or because the customers felt sorry for her. Andi had decided to carry the baby full term but was definitely giving it up for adoption. At night, when she lay down completely exhausted, the baby would kick furiously. She had lost track of how many times she'd cried herself to sleep.

* * * * *

Laurie and Dale sat in stunned silence.

"We've found a baby for you," said Pastor Koby. "A pastor friend of mine knows of a young woman giving her baby up for adoption."

Laurie just sat as Dale began to ask questions.

"I'm sorry, Dale. Because of privacy issues, I can't tell you the mother's name, where she's from, or anything else, other than the fact that she's Caucasian, healthy, and comes from a good Christian family."

Laurie whispered, "Is it a girl or a boy?"

"I don't know that either." Pastor Koby laughed. "I know the baby's due in a few days. If you decide you want this child, it'll be here in your arms next week."

Laurie and Dale looked at each other and reached for each other's hands.

"Would you like to pray about it and get back to me?" asked Pastor Koby.

Laurie looked into Dale's eyes.

Dale turned to Pastor Koby and said, "The only thing we need to pray about is whether to buy a crib right now or five minutes from now."

Word quickly got around their church, and three evenings later, Laurie walked into her home to a loud "Surprise!" Dozens of church ladies had come and decorated her living room, and there were piles of gifts wrapped on the dining-room table. Laurie was speechless but thrilled as her mom and sister rushed over to hug her. They sat her in a chair with balloons tied on the back, and the fun began.

As Laurie and Dale hugged the last guest and shut the door, they surveyed their living room.

"The only thing that comes to mind," Dale said, "is exceedingly, abundantly more than we could ever ask or think." Their eyes scanned bottles, nipples, receiving blankets, hats, shoes, sleepers, socks, pacifiers, stuffed animals, baby seats, stroller, bassinet, a high chair, on and on. They were so thoroughly wiped out that they sat on the sofa with their head back.

"This seems surreal," said Laurie.

They went to bed in a daze. Laurie kept her cell phone with her at all times, anxiously awaiting the call. Dale came home from work at 10:30 a.m. He slowly climbed the stairs to see Laurie putting the finishing touches to the nursery. Since they didn't know if it was a girl or boy, she had painted the nursery a sunny yellow with yellow-and-white gingham curtains. They had chosen the name Dakota for a boy and Paige for a girl.

Laurie turned as Dale came into the room. One look at his face, and her heart dropped. Dale walked over to her and said, "The mother decided to keep the baby, Laurie."

Laurie covered her face with her hands and slid to the floor with uncontrollable sobbing.

* * * * *

Isaac loved to garden. He and Becca had planted a garden in the back of his house. The tomatoes were prolific. He had set metal hoops over the plants, and they had grown six feet tall. Each plant yielded a full basket of tomatoes. He had carefully tilled and fertilized the soil. He had brought in many loads of topsoil and tilled over and over. The ground was rich and loamy. It produced carrots that were ten inches long and sugar sweet. Becca called them her carrot cookies. The peppers, cucumbers, squash, and zucchini were so abundant he could barely keep up with it. He planted some pumpkins and gourds for Becca. Next year, he would add corn. His parents had a garden in Mississippi, where he learned from a small boy how to plow, plant, and weed. He had loved being in 4-H and had won blue ribbons for his produce.

"Daddy?"

"Yes, Bec?"

"Can we have a sleep out tonight?"

He looked into her sweet face as she excitedly pranced from foot to foot. "Sure, we can!"

"Yay! Yay!" she said, jumping up and down. "And we can find the dippers and Neptune and wave at the moon and wave at Mommy in heaven."

Isaac's eyes teared as he watched her run excitedly around the garden.

"Bring me the wagon, bebop. Let's get this produce boxed up and ready to share."

"Okay, Daddy, I'll bring it right over." Becca pulled her red wagon over and helped Isaac with the buckets of squash and cucumbers.

"Who are we sharing with this time?"

"We're going to take this batch to Abby's grandparents."

"Oh, good, I love Grandma Esther."

* * * * *

Isaac took the doors and roof off the jeep in preparation for an evening ride up the mountain with Abby. He wanted to take her to a certain spot that was perfect to watch the sunset. The crickets were in full force by the time he pulled into Abby's driveway. He saw her standing in the side yard. He eased up behind her and put his hands on her waist. Andi whirled around, standing nose to nose with Isaac. Isaac's eyes were closed as he gently kissed her for the first time. Abby heard their voices as she looked out the living-room window in time to witness the kiss. She knocked furiously on the window as Andi and Isaac looked over at her.

Isaac jumped back and said, "Why didn't you tell me it was you?"

"You didn't give me a chance!" Andi said, laughing.

Abby stormed outside and said, "What do you think you're doing? Is that your idea of a joke because I don't think it's very funny."

Isaac said, "It was an accident, Abby. Surely you know me better by now than to think I would do this on purpose."

Abby looked from Andi to Isaac.

Andi laughed and said, "Oh, Abby, for goodness' sake, I'm not trying to steal your man. He thought I was you."

"Even after you turned around?"

"His eyes were closed."

"So you let him kiss you."

"Abby, it was like a nanosecond before I could even react. And speaking of reacting, I think you're way overreacting."

"Well, maybe it's because I've been down this road with you before, Andi."

Andi stormed off as Abby said, "Isaac, I understand it was an accident, but I'm not in the mood to go riding now."

He watched her walk back in the house. He stood shaking his head, got back in his jeep, and drove off. Abby sniffled as a tear dripped off her chin onto her book she had been trying to read for the last half hour. She felt miserable as she put the book aside. *I wish I hadn't overreacted*, she thought miserably. *Now I feel foolish and embarrassed.*

* * * * *

Victoria was typing as fast she could. She kept glancing at the clock, willing it to be 5:00 p.m. Not that she had any weekend plans, but her neck and shoulders were burning with fatigue, and she was tired.

"Well, for goodness sake, will you look at this?" said Aubrey.

Aubrey pulled an envelope out of her purse and waved it in Victoria's direction. Laughing, she said, "I never even cashed my paycheck last week. Isn't that funny? I forgot all about it."

Victoria smiled and busied herself with her files. Aubrey was always bragging about money, bragging about her social life, bragging about her shopping sprees. She knew Victoria was barely making it and relished in making her feel badly about it.

Her day finally came to an end. Victoria was relieved to climb into her rusted Ford Pinto and drive home. Home was a third-floor apartment on Elmwood Avenue. Victoria scooped her mail from her box and wearily climbed the three stories to her hot stuffy apartment. She turned the key and tossed her purse on the table. She kicked off her shoes and settled into her recliner. It was one luxury she had permitted herself on her very tight budget. Her tiny efficiency apartment was just big enough for a two-burner stove, small fridge and sink, her twin bed and dresser, a small desk and chair, three-tiered plantstand, and a recliner. Victoria was grateful to have her own space even if it was small. She had tried renting with roommates in the past, and it had been disastrous both times. One roommate was always making excuses not to pay her half of the rent. The second one was constantly bringing people home all hours of the night and day. They would eat all the groceries, leave the kitchen a wreck; and once, Victoria came home to find someone actually asleep in her bed. That was the last straw. This efficiency was within her budget, and she appreciated her privacy. It was a bit cold in the winter and too hot and stuffy in summer, but she made do.

Victoria looked through her mail. Most of it was junk. She flipped through the flyers and sale ads, but at the bottom of the pile was a letter addressed to her from an attorney firm: Barnes & Hutchinson. She opened the letter and began to read. She sat up and read it again. She held the letter on her lap and stared into space, trying to comprehend the legalese.

Victoria's father died when she was sixteen years old. She and her mother moved to an apartment over top of Huntsberry's shoe store. When Victoria was nineteen, her mother died suddenly of a brain aneurysm. Her mother had a small insurance policy, but after the funeral expenses were paid, there was less than $5,000 left for Victoria to live on. Victoria was able to find an office job and had been on her own since.

The letter from Barnes & Hutchinson said her father's oldest sister had passed and had willed her house to her. Victoria was stunned beyond comprehension. She was saddened she didn't get word earlier, or she would have gone to the funeral, but her name was not on her aunt's emergency call list.

Victoria's Aunt Mazie had been quite a character in her day. It was heartbreaking that she had gotten dementia. In her younger years, she was eccentric but very precious. She wore thick Coke-bottle glasses and dyed her hair chestnut brown. She wore it in a beehive piled high on top of her head. She always wore dresses and usually had on at least three necklaces over top of each other. She loved pink rouge and wore it liberally. She was not quite five feet tall, barely a hundred pounds soaking wet, and everyone loved her. She could quote dozens of poems by heart, and her dining-room table was set with her good china at all times. Her home was a large quintessential Victorian three-story house with a turret and carved fretwork at the top arches. Victoria remembered the polished banister on the staircase. She had always yearned to slide down that bannister as a child. The most prominent memory was that nearly every room in the house was pink. Aunt Mazie loved pink and loved to paint. Roses

COME TO THE RIVER

were her specialty. There were dozens of pictures of roses all over the walls.

Victoria shook her head sure that some mistake had been made. But there was only one way to find out. She would make an appointment with the attorney and get to the bottom of this startling letter.

Her thoughts were interrupted by a knock on her door. She peeped through the hole and recognized her neighbor. Victoria opened the door.

"Hello, darling," the neighbor said.

"Hello, Mrs. Anderson," Victoria said, hugging her tightly.

Mrs. Anderson had been a neighbor and dear friend. She had often made dinner for Victoria, and they had had wonderful talks in the evenings. Mrs. Anderson was lonely, and Victoria welcomed her friendship with open arms. Victoria had learned so many life lessons and practical teaching from her. She taught her to knit a wool cap and scarf for winter, how to plant a small fragrant herb garden out her kitchen window, how to can vegetables and make jelly, how to stretch a dollar, and best of all, she had shared her secret recipes with her. They had spent many a lonely evening chatting and praying together.

"Well, dear, I wanted to see if you'd like to have my Victrola and my television set. My daughter is coming for me next weekend. I'm moving in with her to take care of my grandbaby while she and her husband work."

Victoria quickly turned her head, pretending to straighten the potted plants, but Mrs. Anderson saw her tears. She held out her arms as Victoria cried on her shoulder.

"Forgive me, Mrs. Anderson. I'm so happy for you. Truly, I am. Your daughter's family will be so blessed. But I'll miss you so much," she blubbered, hugging her again.

Mrs. Anderson was crying too and said, "I wish you could come with me, sweetheart."

Victoria laughed and said, "I'll be fine. You know I will. You've just been so dear to me, and yes, I would love to have your Victrola and TV. Thank you so much. But are you sure you want to give up? That old Victrola is surely an antique and may be worth quite a bit."

"No, darling, they have plenty, and I want to bless you. I also brought something else to give you. It's so you will always remember me."

"As if I'd ever forget you," said Victoria, smiling warmly into Mrs. Anderson's eyes.

Mrs. Anderson handed her a small flat box. Victoria opened it to find a delicate white linen handkerchief with tiny purple violets. The initials VLA were stitched in the corner.

"Oh, Mrs. Anderson, how lovely. Why, these are my initials. How did you know my middle name?" she asked, pleasantly surprised.

"I didn't." Mrs. Anderson laughed. "I stitched those initials when I was a girl. They're my initials too. My name is Virginia Lee Andrews. My married name was Anderson, so they always fit. What is your full name, dear?"

"My name is Victoria Lynnette Ambrose. This is so sweet, Mrs. Anderson. I'll treasure it always."

"We've had some great talks, haven't we?" said Mrs. Anderson.

They stood in companionable silence for a few minutes.

"Will you write to me?" asked Mrs. Anderson.

"Of course, I will. Is there anything I can do to help you pack?" Victoria asked.

"No, I don't really have that much, you know, and my son-in-law will to see to everything. He'll deliver the things to your apartment next Saturday."

Victoria decided against sharing the attorney's letter with Mrs. Anderson. *I'd better check it out first before I embarrass myself. It's probably a mistake anyway,* she thought.

After Mrs. Anderson left, Victoria couldn't help thinking about the possibilities. Then reality set in. Even if it were true, she knew she couldn't afford to keep the house with taxes and upkeep and heat. But maybe she could sell it. "Stop it," she said to herself. She made herself get busy gathering her laundry for the trek to the laundromat.

Victoria's head was spinning as she walked to her car after meeting with Barnes & Hutchinson. Her Aunt Mazie had, in fact, not only left the homeplace, but there was over $760,000 in the estate as well. As the only living relative, Victoria had received an inheritance. She was numb as she climbed into her car, too overwhelmed to think. She was so thankful she had taken the next day off. She impulsively decided right then to go see her property. She raced home to pack an overnight bag, glad for the opportunity to spend a long weekend in the Shenandoah Valley. Nine hours later, she drove slowly down Melrose Avenue, trying to recognize the area. She saw the house and drew in her breath. It was as beautiful as she remembered. The house was three stories and sat on a slight knoll. It was love at first sight. She didn't realize she was crying as her eyes drank in the beauty and detail. It had a wraparound porch, and the windows were wide and plentiful with beautiful shutters. She walked up the walk, her eyes drinking in every detail. She turned the key in the huge wooden door with a stained glass transom and stepped over the threshold that led her into a wide hall, oak-paneled and floored. The electricity had been turned off, but she could still see well enough to look around. The furniture had been covered with white slip covers sitting on thick floral carpets, and the large windows were covered with thick draperies and wooden shutters.

The dark shadows gave the place an eerie look, but Victoria wasn't afraid. To the right was a large dining room with a built-in china closet and large bay window. In the middle of the room sat a massive dining table. It would easily fit sixteen people. She looked closer, and the wood appeared to be mahogany sitting on thick carved legs with claw feet. It was scratched from many years of use, and the wood finish was marred and dull, but Victoria could see beyond the surface. The room had high ceilings and faded floral wallpaper peeling at the edges. Across the hall to the left was another large room with a high oak-beamed ceiling. There were two arched windows with deep window seats, perfect for cushions and cozy pillows. There was an immense fireplace in the middle with built-in bookshelves on each side. Her heart skipped a beat as she squinted her eyes in the dim light. She walked to the corner and pulled the sheet back. There sat an antique Steinway piano. She gingerly sat down on the round wooden stool and tenderly placed her hands on the yellowed keys. She began to play an old hymn from memory. The rich tones filled the house. She continued down the long hall to the kitchen. The floor was flagstone, and the appliances were very old. Although fascinated, Victoria's heart sank at how much it would cost to renovate. Her mind started whirling with figures. She would have to hire someone to check everything out. She felt inadequate as she wondered if the plumbing would need to be replaced and if the roof and foundation were solid. She sighed as she knew there was no way she could afford to make it livable, and even if she could, how could she afford to live in this huge place alone, not to mention repairs and taxes? *I guess I'll have to sell it*, she thought sadly. *But how could I possibly let such an heirloom go? It would break my heart.*

Most of the rooms were too dark to get a good look, but she was thrilled with what she saw. An hour later, she was explaining her plight to the electric company. The clerk was impatiently explaining to Victoria that it was absolutely impossible to have her electricity turned on that day. The supervisor walked over with a beaming smile.

"Excuse me. I couldn't help overhearing your conversation. I knew Mazie McIntyre. She attended my church at Living Waters Fellowship. I'm Sally Edwards."

Victoria warmly shook her hand and said, "I'm Victoria Ambrose. It's so nice to meet you. As you're probably aware, my aunt recently passed, and I inherited her wonderful home. To be honest with you, I found out just, and frankly, I'm a bit overwhelmed. I immediately drove here to see the house, but it's difficult to see inside with no lights. I'm only here until Sunday afternoon for this trip. Do you know how long it would be before the lights could be turned on?"

Mrs. Edwards said, "You inherited the Belair House? Oh, I'm so happy for you."

Victoria said, "I've never heard it referred to as the Belair House. What does that mean?"

"Sharon said that house was built in the 1800s, and during that era, people named their homes. Miss Mazie told me her grandfather built it and named it the Belair House for his wife. Wait right here. Let me see what I can do."

Victoria paced back and forth excitedly, and in a very few minutes, Sally returned with a thumbs-up.

"I called in a favor for you. If you'll just complete this form and pay the fee, your lights should be on in about two hours."

Victoria hugged her. "Oh, Mrs. Edwards, thank you so much."

"It's my pleasure, dear, and please call me Sally. Will you be moving here?"

"I don't have solid plans yet. I haven't had time to think things through."

"If you decide to stay, please let me know. I'd love to invite you for dinner. Your Aunt Mazie was a good friend and a fine Christian lady. She was very loved and respected in our church."

"Thank you, Sally. I promise to let you know."

Victoria eased down into the luxuriously large claw-foot tub, exhausted after a long weekend of treasure finding in her newly inherited home. After much soul searching and prayer, she had decided to move into the house. She wouldn't receive her inheritance money for sixty days, but she had frugally saved some money that she could subsist on. She didn't have a solid plan yet, but knew she wanted to live there for the present. She loved the Shenandoah Valley and had wonderful memories visiting her Aunt Mazie as a child. She had always hoped to relocate here, so this was her golden opportunity.

Victoria shut her eyes as the steamy hot water eased her aching muscles. She had been thrilled to find most of the furniture still serviceable. It would take a lot of work to tackle the dust, much more than she could handle herself. She would inquire about cleaning companies. Her greatest treasures were the boxes of photos, letters, quilts, and framed cross-stitched pictures all over the house. She hadn't even been in the attic or basement yet other than to peek in to see it filled with delightful treasures. Her mind was racing with ideas. Maybe she could open a B&B. As she relaxed in the hot water, she realized how she longed for a family. *I could open a boardinghouse for other people who are alone, and we could all be a family together.* As she rested in the hot water, her thoughts tumbled faster than she could organize them. If she were to remodel this place, she would need to hire carpenters, electricians, plumbers. The list seemed staggering. But she would pace herself and seek counsel from a godly friend of hers who had a good business head. She would try to do as much work as she could herself.

Victoria wanted to go to church. She hadn't brought dress clothes to wear, but her casual clothes were clean. She had spotted a church steeple from an upstairs bedroom window and decided to check it out, hoping they wouldn't mind her appearance. She felt refreshed from her hot bath and excitedly headed out the door. Her heart overflowed with gratitude as she walked down the sidewalk, the sun warm on her face. The church bells were ringing as the church came into view. The signboard read "Living Water Fellowship." She timidly walked up the steps and was warmly greeted by a husband-and-wife team. They welcomed her and gave her a visitor's packet. She thanked them and slipped into the nearest pew. She anxiously looked around and was immediately relieved to see people dressed every way imaginable. Some had on suits and dresses, but the vast majority were quite casual. She was thankful she wouldn't stand out. Her eyes drank in the beauty of the church with the high ceilings and beautiful tapestries on the walls. Suddenly the choir stood up and began to sing a lively hand-clapping praise song. Everyone stood and joined in. The words flashed up on the wall, and Victoria felt herself drawn in as she too began to sing along to the simple melody. It felt good to be part of this group worshipping so freely. She was thankful to be unknown yet felt very much a part of this body of believers.

The pastor told the congregation to greet one another. The woman to Victoria's left shook her hand and, smiling, said, "Good morning, dear. I'm Anna."

Before Victoria could reply, a man in front of her turned and said, "Mornin', darlin', God bless you."

Victoria smiled warmly and said, "Thank you, sir, the same to you."

Victoria looked up to see Sally Edwards coming toward her. "I'm so glad you're here, Victoria. What a lovely surprise."

Before Victoria could blink, Sally said to several people around her, "This is Mazie McIntyre's niece."

Many heads turned with warm smiles, and before everyone had sat down, over a dozen people had greeted her. She was a bit stunned at how easy that was. No probing questions, no one put her on the spot. It was actually fun, like speed friends. She shook her head slightly, thinking this was a most unusual place of worship. At the end of the service, they announced that a new ministry for singles would be launched the following Saturday evening for a barbecue. Victoria felt a wave of excitement go through her. This was a fascinating church, and she would definitely visit again.

* * * * *

Isaac smiled at the Hallmark card Abby had mailed him. They hadn't spoken for three days, and he missed her terribly. They had planned a date that evening, and he was looking forward to it. He picked her up promptly at six, and they went to dinner at the Corner Shop. As they ate their pizza, they shared their salvation stories and tidbits about their lives. They laughed easily and enjoyed each other's presence so much conversation wasn't even necessary. The next weeks were magical. Isaac was romantic. He wrote Abby notes and sent her flowers. Abby enjoyed cooking for him and Becca. They had long rides in his truck with Becca in tow. Becca had fallen in love with Abby and cried at night when she had to leave her. Abby got through her workweeks looking forward to their weekends spent together. They realized they had the same taste in music. Today they were going for a picnic by themselves. Becca was at a sleepover. Isaac brought the picnic lunch this time. The worship music was turned up loud, and their windows were open. They were smiling and riding up a winding mountain road. The sun was filtering through the trees. The climb was getting steeper when he said, "Okay, we're almost here. Close your eyes. I'd like to surprise you."

She obediently closed her eyes as the truck came to a stop. She heard him get out and open her door. "Keep your eyes closed. Walk with me."

She took his arm and walked slowly along. He stopped and turned her around. "Okay, open your eyes."

Abby gasped in delight as she saw they were on the tip-top of the mountain with an overlook of the valley. The view was magnificent. The leaves were changing colors, and you could see for miles around.

"Oh my goodness, this is amazing. Where are we?" She turned a full circle and saw there was a large building with walls mostly made of glass.

"This used to be a restaurant, but many years ago, there was a fire, and it closed. The owners never rebuilt."

"What a shame. The views are spectacular. I'm sure it must have been very popular in its time."

"Yes, I would think so, although the road up here isn't that easy to travel even in good weather. It seems a shame for someone's dream to die. They probably put their heart and soul into this place."

She turned back to look down at the valley. "I want to grab my camera. This place is breathtaking."

They grabbed hands as he led through some trails, pointing out different trees and plants. He pulled some needles off a low-lying branch and rolled it in his hands to crush the needles. Cupping his hands together, he held it up to her face.

"Smell this."

"Oh my, it's heavenly. What is it?"

"This is a sage tree."

She could hear water as they were walking the trail. Around the bend was a small waterfall. There was barely any sunlight as it was secluded by branches and limbs draping over the water. It was cool and smelled fresh like damp earth and fragrant sap from the sage and pine trees. He led her carefully down the steep bank. He pointed to a large flat rock jutting out of the side of the mountain.

"If we stand on that ledge, it will put us behind the waterfall."

They carefully maneuvered around and stepped gingerly on the ledge. They inched their way behind the waterfall. They were standing so close they could feel a bit of the spray in their face. Abby reached out and put her fingers in the water. The light was filtering through, making rainbows on the rocks behind them.

"I love the way it smells in here. Like clean damp earth and fresh ozone."

Isaac reached for her hand and said, "I feel the presence of the Lord in here."

Abby's heart nearly burst with love for this man. He led her by the hand back up the embankment to a huge Beech tree. He took out his pocket knife and carved their initials in the trunk. He winked at her and said, "Someday we'll show that to our grandkids."

Isaac was spreading out the quilt on the ground.

"Where's your picnic basket?"

He laughed and said, "My picnic cardboard box is in the back of the truck."

He laid out paper plates and some plastic containers, a bag of Fritos, two cans of cold Orange Sunkist.

"Okay, what do we have here?" she asked.

The first container held sliced cooked venison tenderloin; the next container had two whole pickles and two hardboiled eggs. The next container held what appeared to be some sort of cheese dip. He brought out the plastic knives and forks and said, "This is queso cheese dip. I made it with cheese and spicy tomatoes with green chilies. I melted it all together, and you dip your Fritos and venison in it. It's good. Would you like to try it? I think it's only fair to warn you that it's very addictive."

She took a bite and closed her eyes in ecstasy. She bit into the dill pickle and said, "This is, without a doubt, the best dinner ever."

Isaac looked pleased and proud. When they'd finished, he said, "Would you care for a kiss?"

She raised her eyebrows at him, thinking of him kissing her sister.

"Our first kiss didn't go exactly as planned. So I'll ask you again, would you like a kiss?"

Before Abby could react, he held out a Hershey's Kiss. She laughed, and she took it from him. "So where did the venison come from?"

He smiled and said, "Some of my patients don't have much money, so they pay me in trade."

She laughed and said, "Oh my. Does that happen often?"

He shook his head no but said, "When I know they are truly indigent, I usually suggest a barter. It helps them keep their pride and not feel like they're taking charity."

Isaac had positioned the blanket on a slight hill so they could lean back and see the overlook. Abby lay back on the quilt with her arms behind her head. Isaac lay down beside her. They turned on their sides, facing each other. Isaac turned Abby over and pulled her back up against his chest. They spooned looking at the gorgeous fall leaves in total comfort. A few minutes later, Abby turned over to face him. The sun felt warm as they chatted easily for an hour. Isaac leaned in for a gentle kiss. Abby's heart raced as he passionately kissed her again. As they lay with their arms wrapped around each other, they felt a rush of abandonment and freedom. The leaves were gently falling around them, and the temperature was perfect. They continued to kiss until passion began to sweep them into a dangerous place. Isaac's breath was ragged as he abruptly sat up. He stood up, frustrated, running his hand through his hair.

"We need to stop."

Abby said, "Yes, we do." She shivered as she stood up.

They stood arm in arm, looking over the valley. He hugged her and said, "I don't know if I could ever stop again, Abby."

She nodded. "Thank you. Thank you, Isaac."

"God gets the glory, Abby. It truly wasn't me. If I had my way, I'd make love to you right now with no hesitation. And not because I'm worked up either. It's because I'm in love with you. I love everything about you. I love the way you laugh. I love your brown eyes. I love your compassion for your patients. I love your sense of humor. I love your strong, uncomplicated faith. Will you marry me? Would you help me raise Becca? She already adores you, Abby. I can't live without you."

Abby was breathless as she nodded. His shout of happiness echoed down the valley.

"I have to go to a teaching conference next week."

"Where is it located?"

"I have to fly to Chicago for four days."

"Who will keep Becca?"

"I have an excellent babysitter, but this will be the longest I've ever been away from her."

"I wish I was off. I'd keep her. Would it help if I visited with her in the evenings?"

"I wouldn't want you to have to jump hoops, Abby."

"It's not jumping hoops, Isaac. I love Becca, and I happen to know she loves me."

Isaac took her hand and said, "Yes, she does. Almost as much as her father does. We need to set a date. We'll look at the calendar when we get home."

* * * * *

Victoria's employer was very surprised to read her resignation letter.

"We're sorry to see you go, Victoria. You've done a great job for us, but I must say, this seems very sudden. What are your plans?"

Victoria was not willing to share her personal life and especially the details of her inheritance. She had a satisfactory working relationship with her employer and coworkers, but they distanced themselves a bit from her, and Victoria had learned to guard her heart where they were concerned.

"I'm moving to Northern Virginia. Thank you for the opportunities you've given me here. I appreciate it." There was something in Victoria's quiet assurance that kept her supervisor from probing deeper. Victoria prayed Thanksgiving prayers all day in her heart, so thankful for her new beginnings.

Victoria looked around her apartment, realizing how little she had to pack. She could get everything in one small truck. She jumped when the phone rang. She was surprised to receive a call from Mrs. Anderson's daughter, explaining rather curtly that her mother had had a stroke and was left partially paralyzed on her left side.

"We'll be placing Mother in a nursing next Tuesday."

"Oh my, I'm so sorry. Is she not able to care for herself? What is her prognosis?"

Her daughter was cool and defensive. Victoria was able to find out which nursing home before her daughter hung up. Victoria cried as she finished packing, asking the Lord to comfort and heal Mrs. Anderson.

She gave one last look around at her apartment that had been her home for the last eight years. She felt no emotional connection, especially since Mrs. Anderson had moved. But she was grateful for her humble home that God had provided her. She drove resolutely out of town with high hopes for a new beginning.

* * * * *

Esther awakened with a start and glanced at the bedside clock. The red numbers read 3:00 a.m. Her spirit was immediately on the alert. She recognized the Holy Spirit tapping her for intercession. Someone needed prayer. She got up and went to the living room and began to pray.

* * * * *

Renee McCormick looked at the clock for the tenth time. Her stomach was in a knot as she fretted that dinner would be dried out and that there would be no time to start over before Michael came home. He always demanded his dinner hot and ready to eat, and she had tasted his punishment when it wasn't exactly what he expected. He was already an hour and twenty minutes late.

Wringing the dish towel between her hands, she dropped to one knee, carefully examining the table and counters, making sure there was not one speck of debris or fingerprints. As she heard the garage door open, she nervously dished up the dinner on the pre-warmed plate. Her heart raced when she heard his measured steps. As he stepped into the kitchen, she glanced at him and saw he was in no mood to be trifled with.

She sat his plate down and poured his iced tea. He cruelly demanded that she eat every meal with him. It gave him sick pleasure to torment her at every given opportunity. Her stomach churned acid, raising bile in her throat. She quietly sat down. He took one bite. He slowly chewed, scowling at the plate. Before she could blink, he hurled the plate across the room, shattering it against the stove. Food spewed against the cabinets and counters.

Renee squeezed her eyes shut, tensing for his fit of fury. He grabbed the edge of the kitchen table with both hands, tossing it out of the way. He backhanded her across the face with brute strength, splitting her lip, then body-slammed her against the refrigerator. He held her by her throat, spitting in her face.

"This food is garbage," he screamed, causing veins to bulge in his neck and forehead. He drove his fist into her stomach, knocking the breath out of her. She fell to the floor in agony, curling into a tight ball. He kicked her in the ribs and stormed out of the kitchen.

Renee slowly moved her head, trying to focus. She gingerly pulled herself up, holding on to the kitchen chair lying on its side. She tiptoed to the garage door and quietly eased it open a fraction of an inch and saw that Michael's car was gone. She wept with relief as she staggered to the bathroom. She had to get the mess cleaned up before he returned.

* * * * *

Angela's neck burned with fatigue. She rolled her shoulders and sighed. She was on a deadline for this wedding cake, and tired or not, it had to get done. This was a three-layer cake. She had stacked it, crumb iced it, and draped the fondant over it, attached the ribbon, flowers, and bling. She painstakingly piped the last touches of scroll-work and stepped back to view her work. *Genius, absolute genius*, she thought. She smiled, knowing she had done a superb job. The cake was stunning, and the bride would be quite happy with it.

"Use this spatula when you lift it up," she said. "I've seen too many fingers slip and jab into the side of the cake. This small container is more icing just in case that happens. Take a coat with you. You have to keep the air-conditioner on in the car no matter how cold you get. And when you arrive, if you have far to walk, go ask for a cart. Trust me, you don't want to drop this cake, or you'll be in big trouble!" Her cell phone rang as she was giving last-minute instructions to her helper. Angela waved to her as she backed out the driveway and drove off.

"Hello, Angela?"

"Jenna."

"Todd and I are going to the movies tonight, and Todd's cousin is in town, visiting. Todd wants to know if you'd like to go. We'll make a double."

Angela was silent a few seconds. "Jenna," Angela said, "you know how I feel about blind dates. Not interested, but thanks anyway."

"Oh, Angela, please don't say no! I've met James. He's gentle and sweet."

"Has he been married?" Angela asked.

"Yes, he's divorced."

"Why were they divorced?"

"I don't know," Jenna replied thoughtfully. "I didn't ask."

"No, Jenna. I don't go out with men I don't know."

"Oh, Angela, come on."

"No. I have to go."

She hung up and crossed her arms over her chest. She immediately thought of her father and how secretly abusive he was. He was Mr. Wonderful to everyone else but calculating and cruel to her and her mother. One month after she turned eighteen, her mother had helped her escape. They had planned it for a year. Angela had begged her mother to leave with her, but her mother felt it would be too dangerous for them to leave together.

Angela had won an award for a science project in school. She had carefully grown a mold sample under glass and had won the trophy in the science fair. Her father had a picture of the two of them smiling at the camera holding the trophy. The whole mantel was filled with "happy" family photos.

For his birthday, she baked him a cheesecake from scratch. She took a toothpick and scraped a bit of the mold from the project into the batter. It did its work well, and he vomited violently for hours. She had been able to crawl out the bedroom window with money she saved from babysitting and went straight to the bus depot. She rode six days and nights and started her life over across the country. The final part of the plan was getting her mother to safety. Angela was to write "General Delivery" with the town and state where she was hiding on a postcard. She would mail it to a friend in Wichita, Kansas, and that friend would forward it to Angela. Angela would send a post back so they could connect.

* * * * *

Jonathan Avery hung up the phone, disgusted with himself for cutting the power line. He had called the electric company to let them know he had accidentally cut into the line while using his backhoe. He decided to drive to the end of the road to apologize to the neighbors and let them know the power would return in a few hours. He had never met these neighbors, but he had seen them come and go in their vehicle. He knocked on their door and heard soft footsteps. After a couple of minutes, he knocked again.

"Who's there?" said a soft voice.

"Hello, I'm Jonathan Avery. I live down the road and wanted to let you know I accidentally cut your power line with my backhoe. I'm sorry, but I called the electric company, and they said the power should return in a few hours."

Renee cracked the door. Jonathan immediately noticed bruises on her neck and wrists. He looked her in the eye, and she quickly looked away.

"Thank you," she said softly.

He said, "Is there anything I can do for you?"

She became agitated and said, "No, thank you. And please, as much as I appreciate it, please don't visit here again. My husband is…is wary of strangers and won't be polite. Again, thank you."

She shut the door, and he heard her bolt it from the inside.

Jonathan was immediately on the alert. He assumed she was an abused wife. Make that a terrified abused wife. He also knew she was on the other side of the door, waiting for him to leave.

He quietly said, "I'm sliding my card under your door. If you ever need help, ma'am, you can trust me. Please don't be afraid of me. I'm a God-fearing man, and I'll help if you'll let me."

He slid his card under the door and got back in his truck. As he was backing out of the driveway, he saw the curtain move slightly and knew she was watching him. He prayed for her as he drove home. *Lord, do you want me to get involved here?* Instantly, an idea dropped in his mind.

* * * * *

Esther awakened for the second night at exactly 3:00 a.m. She got up and began to worship the Lord, waiting for him to guide her prayers. A spirit of intercession began to move on her, and she prayed in the spirit until the burden lifted. She looked at the clock. It was 4:50 a.m. She had been praying almost two hours. She crawled back under the covers and was sound asleep in moments.

* * * * *

The prayer team met an hour before service every Sunday at Living Water Fellowship. Esther was the prayer leader. The prayer team was small in number but powerful in authority. These people knew how to take care of kingdom business. Esther shared that the Lord had awakened her to pray at three o'clock every morning for three solid weeks.

"I don't know who I'm praying for," she said. "But I know it's serious."

She asked the prayer team to join her and intercede for this situation. They spent the next thirty minutes praying together.

Abby approached Esther after the church service was over.

"Hello, Miss Esther. Do you have time to talk with me a moment? If not, it can wait."

"Of course, Abby. I have all the time in the world. Here, have a seat. What's on your mind, darling?"

"I'd like to ask you something, but you need to promise to be honest with me."

Esther smiled and nodded. "I promise."

Abby said, "I was wondering if you might have time to…well, to help me learn to pray more effectively. But if you don't have time, I totally understand. Also I wanted to share something really personal with you. Remember when Isaac rescued me when I fell in the river?"

"Oh yes, I certainly do."

"Well, I had an experience with Jesus, and I'm feeling it's time to share it. I feel a little insecure, but I was hoping you could help me find the right scriptures and maybe help me be confident sharing my testimony."

Esther laughed in delight and said, "It would be my absolute pleasure. Why don't you come over to my home this afternoon about 3:00 p.m.?"

"Okay, I'd love to. I'll see you then."

Esther watched Abby walk away, praying as she went. *Thank you, Lord, for this grand opportunity to teach the next generation.*

* * * * *

Angela was in line at the post office when she heard her name called. She turned to find a smiling couple coming her way. It was the bride and groom she had baked the wedding cake for.

"Angela, I'm so glad to see you!"

"Nora, John, nice to see you too. How's married life?"

They both beamed, and Nora said, "Just great! We just wanted to say what a wonderful job you did on our cake. Not only was it lavishly gorgeous, it was also delicious. We got so many compliments on it. Thank you so much."

"Oh, I'm so glad you liked it." Angela beamed.

"We did. We definitely did!" Nora beamed. "I'll e-mail you some pictures the photographer took when we were cutting it. It really shows off the detail work!"

"That will be great!"

They hugged, and Angela turned to get back in line. As Nora and John walked away, Nora impulsively turned back and said, "Angela, my church, Living Water Fellowship, is having a ladies' tea next Saturday. We're all to invite a special friend to come with us to this event. I would love for you to come with me! Would you happen to be free?"

Angela knew without checking her calendar that next Saturday morning was free. It was a very rare thing for her to have a Saturday off. She was about to turn her down when Nora said, "It only lasts a couple hours. We have a guest speaker and music, and it ends with a luncheon. We only have one a year, and it's really special. I hope you can come with me. It'll be fun."

Angela found herself saying yes. As she stood in line to mail her package, she wondered why she had agreed to go. It was so out of character for her to go anywhere with people she didn't know well. But she felt excited to get to do something different. She had virtually no personal life and no real friends, just some acquaintances. She suddenly felt light and glad. She had never been to a tea and had rarely ever been inside a church. She was nervous and wondered if she'd feel out of place and what she should wear.

* * * * *

Michael was working on his laptop while Renee was washing the dishes. He had come home from work in a brooding mood. He had eaten his dinner without complaint and was working over some business papers in the den. Renee was thankful for the quiet, but the eerie calmness made her wary and nervous. Without warning, Michael grabbed her by her hair and jerked her off her feet, her toes barely touching the floor.

"Why did you open the door to a stranger, Renee?"

The pain was searing, and it took all she had not to cry out. He jerked her hard and said in a steely cold voice, "Answer me."

She could feel his hot breath on her face. "It...it was the neighbor. He came to let us know he had cut the power lines with his backhoe by accident. And he said the power company would get the electricity back on in a few hours."

"You know you're not to answer the door. You're wondering how I knew, aren't you?" Michael laughed and continued coolly, "I'm watching you, my love. Don't ever forget that."

He shoved her against the door and walked off. She hugged herself, rocking back and forth in pain. Rubbing her head, silent tears ran down her cheeks as she saw a chunk of hair came out in her hands. She prayed he didn't know about the business card. She had memorized Jonathan's name and number and burned the card and flushed the ashes. But it gave her hope. She definitely had a kernel of hope.

* * * * *

Jonathan had been watching Renee's house through his binoculars in his tree stand. He had witnessed her husband smack her around, and it made him livid, but he knew he had to be calculated and patient if he was to help her. If he went in too soon, it could cost her, her life.

Jonathan had grown up in the mountains. His father and older brothers taught him to shoot when he was a young boy. He had spent a happy childhood running through the woods. He was raised in a family that trapped and hunted and fished. He went to college and was advised by a wonderful professor to major in political science, and that degree landed him a great job in the CIA. Through working in intelligence, Jonathan had accumulated a great deal of experience in electronics, as well as learning to trust his instincts. That experience, along with the power of the Holy Spirit, made Jonathan a force to be reckoned with.

He had never married. He had plenty of offers, but he never found the right woman and, more importantly, had never had the release from God to marry. He had a good life and was the Royal Ranger leader at his church. It kept him busy and in shape. The boys in his class loved him, and he loved sowing into their lives. But at this stage of his life, he began to yearn for a life partner.

He had been watching Renee's home long enough to know Michael's pattern. Renee didn't drive. She didn't go anywhere. The only time she came outside was to work in the garden or hang the laundry on the clothesline. Renee lovingly tended her flower garden. It was magnificent with color. Jonathan had tears in his eyes the day he watched Michael rip handfuls of her beautiful flowers up by the roots and kick and stomp through the garden in a rage. He made Renee stand and watch, and he plowed through like a man possessed.

Jonathan had found the hidden cameras outside that Michael had erected to watch every move his wife made. But Jonathan had experience and knew how to get around those cameras. He had slid a note under her door, explaining that he knew she was being abused and offered a way of escape. He assured her he was legit and instructed her to hang a red bandana on the clothesline along with her regular laundry anytime she wanted out; he would keep watch. He knew her laundry day was Tuesday, and this was Tuesday. He had checked every Tuesday for six weeks. As he climbed into his tree stand, he picked up the binoculars to take a look. Adrenaline shot through him like a rocket when he spotted the red cloth.

Jonathan quickly climbed down from the tree stand and ran to his truck. He punched in Pastor's Bob's number, alerting him they would be coming soon. They had a plan in place. Pastor Bob and his wife had contacted another pastor friend across the country in the Shenandoah Valley who would help them with their plan of escape.

Jonathan slammed into her driveway, pointing his laser at the hidden cameras, causing them to pause. He raced to the house, and before he could even get to the door, Renee ran out with two suitcases.

"We have ninety seconds before the cameras come back on. Are you sure this is all you want to take?"

"Yes," she assured him. "Let's go."

They sped down the road. Renee had two black eyes, and her neck was swollen and riddled with bruises.

"I'm taking you to my pastor's house," he said. "They will keep you safe there until time for your bus to leave. They'll send you to a safe house where you'll be protected."

Renee was visibly trembling.

"Why now?" he asked her.

She said, "God spoke to me in a dream. He said he was going to send someone to help me."

Tears came to his eyes. "You're gonna make it, Renee."

He pulled into the driveway at his pastor's house, and the pastor and his wife ran out to meet them.

* * * * *

Angela pulled into Living Water right at 10:00 a.m. Insecurity struck her full force. She could not even make herself get out of the car when Nora opened the church door and walked toward her, smiling.

"I'm so happy you're here. I prayed you would come!"

Angela felt her face heat as she walked up the sidewalk with her. When they walked into the fellowship hall, Angela was delighted with all the beautiful decorations. Each table had a different colored linen tablecloth and tablescape. At her table, the centerpiece was a teapot filled with fresh flowers. Pearls and rose petals were sprinkled throughout. At the front of the room were long tables with dozens of china teacups with matching saucers, as well as platters of fruit, small sandwiches, pastries, and scones. She was relieved that she had dressed up a little. Everyone looked so nice. She was happy to take a seat as the leader welcomed them. Angela tried hard not to cry during the meeting, but the speaker touched her heart deeply. She glanced around and saw many women wiping their eyes. Never had she heard someone speak with such transparency. She prayed with every bit of sincerity at the end when they led the prayer to receive Jesus as Savior and Lord. She had longed for this truth. Peace and joy coursed through her. Tears flowed unchecked. Nora reached over to hug her, and Angela unreservedly hugged her back.

* * * * *

Cherry jumped at the knock at the door. "Jewell," she whispered. Jewell's eyes were huge. "Go hide, quickly! Don't make a sound."

Jewell dashed up the stairs. The door knocker sounded again loudly. Cherry peered through the peephole. Fear flooded through her being.

"Oh my God, it's the SWAT team."

She didn't know whether to be terrified or relieved. She opened the door, and there stood a large black woman in a black T-shirt that had "SWAT" across the front.

"Hello, I'm Inez, and we're here to—"

Before she could finish her sentence, Cherry said, "Please don't kills us, we'll surrender. I have an eight-year-old child here. Please don't shoot us."

Inez said, "Honey, what in the world you talking about?"

Cherry said, "Are you a SWAT team?"

She said, "Yes, but we're not the police SWAT team. We're from Living Water Church, and SWAT stands for 'Sent with a Testimony.' We wanted to share Jesus with you and invite you to church!"

Cherry started crying with relief.

Inez said, "Can I come in, honey?"

Cherry stepped back and let her in.

"What's going on, baby? I'm not gonna hurt you."

Cherry looked into Inez's dark eyes, and before she could change her mind, her story spilled out that the town's bank president had her and an eight-year-old girl who was hiding upstairs captive, and he had repeatedly raped them both.

"What?" Inez gasped. "Dear Jesus, where is that baby girl?"

Cherry called out, "Jewell? Come down, it's okay."

Jewell came down with terrified eyes. Inez gathered them both in her ample arms and patted their backs. "Get your things. We're leaving here right now," Inez decreed.

"No, no, oh God, he'll kill us!"

"No, he won't. Here, we'll help you. Get your things together. I'm taking you home with me right now, and we'll decide what to do."

When Inez got the girls home, she sat them at her kitchen table and fixed them some lunch. They huddled close together, their eyes darting at every noise.

"Now let's make some plans," she said. "I want you to know God loves you so much that He sent me to your house to rescue you. We're going to go to the police for protection."

"No, please, the police already know about us. The bank president, Mr. Pool, pays them a lot of money for them to look the other way. If he finds out, not only will he come after us, he'll hire a hit man to come after you. He'll have you murdered."

"No, baby, ain't nobody gonna murder me. 'Cause the Holy Ghost surrounds me with a shield, glory to God, and He gonna surround you too. Let's start with your names. What's your last name?"

Cherry looked at the floor.

"Honey, listen to me. You're safe. Do you hear me? I ain't gonna let nobody hurt you, and that bank president is going to jail. Mark my words. God sent me to you! My prayer team's been praying for weeks, and I believe you're the reason. God loves you."

Cherry shook her head, tears spilling down her face. "He can't love me. I've done too many bad things."

"Is your real name Cherry?"

"No, ma'am."

"What is it?"

"It's Sharon. Sharon Brown."

"What's this baby's name? Is it Jewell?" Inez asked.

"No, it's Mary Beth."

"Where are your parents?"

"Both of our parents are dead."

"How did you get mixed up in this?"

"I didn't have any money, and this man rescued me in the park and bought me dinner and was so nice. He let me stay here...then things changed, and...and I..." Sharon buried her face in her hands and sobbed.

"And what about this child?"

"She was already here when I came. I don't know how she got here, and she can't remember."

"How old are you, Sharon?"

"I'm eighteen," she replied.

"Why didn't you leave at eighteen?"

"I couldn't leave Mary Beth by herself."

"Lord have mercy. Holy Spirit, help us," Inez whispered. "Do you have any other family?"

"No, ma'am."

Both girls were exhausted from fear. Inez talked them into lying on the bed, and she covered them with a quilt. She said, "I'm not leaving you."

She pulled up a chair next to the bed and began to hum. After a few minutes, she softly started singing "His Eye Is on the Sparrow."

Sharon said, "My grandmother used to sing that."

"Shhh, you just rest now. Everything gonna be okay. My prayer team gonna pray heaven down for you girls. The devil's on the run now, baby." She patted Sharon's hand and said, "Rest now."

When they fell off to sleep, Inez called Esther and filled her in. Esther got the pastor and the other prayer team members together, and they began to pray for wisdom and direction.

* * * * *

Michael stood dumbfounded in shock and disbelief when he entered the house. It was stone quiet, and all the lights were off. Fury made his head pound with pain as adrenaline coursed through him. He became violent and raged through the house like a madman. He kicked things out of his way as he ran from room to room, shouting for Renee. He checked the hidden cameras but saw nothing amiss. He would find her. He would stop at nothing. He would go to any expense to find his wife, and when he did, she would pay for defying him.

* * * * *

Renee was exhausted as she stretched in her seat. Her black eyes were now yellow and green. Her hair was greasy, and her clothes were rumpled from sleeping in them for days. But she breathed a deep breath of peace. She smiled as she looked out the bus window, feeling safe for the first time in many years.

* * * * *

"Would you like me to braid your hair?"

Esther was combing Mary Beth's hair with long, slow strokes. Mary Beth had spent the week with Esther and was finally starting to relax. The first few days, she never left her side. Esther had slept with her, holding her hand. Mary Beth smiled and nodded slightly. She hadn't said two dozen words. After carefully questioning Sharon she found out Mary Beth had never been to school, but Sharon had taught her to read and write. Pastor Bob had contacted his attorney for advice, and they had decided to go to the police, sheriff, state police, the mayor, and the FBI to report what was going on. The local police captain said he knew nothing about the situation. Gerald Pool, the bank president, was arrested that very day. After a search warrant in his home, they seized his computers and files and had enough evidence to put him away for life.

Social Services allowed Esther and Thomas to take temporary custody of Mary Beth. They knew they wouldn't adopt her at their age, but they wanted to minister to her for a while before placing her with strangers. They had arranged for a pediatrician to examine her and made arrangements with a Christian child psychologist. Mary Beth had been through literally years of trauma, and it would take a miracle for her to get straightened out, but Esther and Thomas knew they served a God of miracles. They had laid hands on Mary Beth in her sleep and cast out demonic spirits. They prayed fervently for her inner healing. They had asked God to remove the images and memories from her mind. They had their entire prayer team interceding for her and Sharon both.

Pastor Bob had sent Sharon to a Christian counselor specializing in abuse and trauma, and the church family had showered her with the love of God and truth of His Word. They explained the way of salvation, and she had readily accepted Jesus as her Savior. They had placed her in Victoria Ambrose's Christian boardinghouse, the

Belair House. The church had paid her rent for the next six months, and she was settling in. The church would help her find a job when she was ready. In the meantime, they would look out for her, and she would continue to be mentored and attend weekly Bible studies. Several ladies at the church had taken her under their wing and brought her into their families.

* * * * *

Angela could hardly believe her eyes. There in her stack of mail was a blank postcard with Chicago, Illinois, on it. Angela wept with joy, thanking the Lord over and over.

"Oh God, she's free! She's free!"

She immediately called the local paper in Chicago and placed a personal ad to "General Delivery." It read, "Received your card. Letter to follow."

She had so many plans to make.

"Keep her safe, Lord. Please don't let Dad find us."

Two weeks later, Angela was rolling out fondant icing when she heard the bell on the bakery door tinkle.

"I'll be right out," she called.

She quickly washed her hands and walked from the back room. There stood her beautiful mother. She looked frail and tired, but her eyes were twinkling with delight.

"Mom!" They fell in each other's arms.

"Oh, my baby!" Renee was holding her, touching her face, kissing her face, crying, hugging her. They were laughing and crying.

"Mom, why didn't you call me? I would have come to get you."

"It's too dangerous. Your father is a powerful man with a great deal of money. You know him. He'll stop at nothing to find me. I'm sure he's hired private detectives by now. It's way too dangerous for us to be together. I can't stay, but I wanted to just see you and let you know I'm all right."

"What do you mean you can't stay?" Angela asked. "You're living with me. I'll never be separated from you again!"

"Not right now, it's not safe. The family that helped me in Chicago have arranged for me to stay in someone's home forty-five minutes from here. We can still see each other at times, but we have to be very careful not to leave any trail. You can only call me on a track phone with minutes that you buy. That way, your phone can't be tapped or tracked in any way."

"Mom, that's no existence," Angela said.

"It has to be for now. I have to leave now, but I'll call you. Give me your phone number."

They quickly exchanged numbers, and Renee left, begging Angela not to come out on the sidewalk or follow her.

* * * * *

Pastor Bob was meeting with Dick and Delores Shifflett. They told him they felt the Lord leading them to adopt Mary Beth. They had one daughter, Megan, who was also eight years old. They had been visiting with Mary Beth for weeks. Mary Beth had spent the weekend a few times; it had been an extremely positive experience. Pastor Bob was reminding them all she had been through.

"Right now this might be a honeymoon phase. You do realize she's had no nurturing in her formative years. She's been exposed to so much for such a little girl. She could have nightmares, act out. I'm not trying to discourage you, but I want to make sure you're not going into this with rose-colored glasses. She may need professional counseling."

Dick said, "We realize that, Pastor, but we know God is able, and we're willing. We know God will equip us to handle anything that comes along."

Pastor Bob prayed with them and said he would contact the attorney that would handle the details for them.

* * * * *

Renee was bone-weary of planning every move she made. She longed for peace of mind and to develop some type of normal existence, but she would do whatever it took to keep her daughter safe. She had picked up some houses to clean, and that had worked out very well. She earned enough to pay rent on her weekly hotel room and food. They paid her cash that couldn't be traced.

She jumped when her track phone rang. Her heart raced as she knew they would never call unless it had something to do with Michael or Angela.

"Renee, it's Nancy. I just got word your husband had a stroke. He's dead."

"Are you sure?"

"Yes," Nancy said. "He was identified."

"Thank you for letting me know."

"It's over, Renee. You're safe. You're safe. Let it sink in. You and Angela are safe!"

"Thank you, Nancy. I'm just in a state of shock. I'll call you back when I make some plans."

Renee sat on the sofa, staring into space. *Thank You, God.* She immediately got in the car and drove straight to see Angela.

* * * * *

Megan and Mary Beth were coloring in the backyard.

"I'm glad you're my sister, Megan."

"I'm glad too, Mary Beth."

Mary Beth was adapting well. She loved second grade and was a delight to the family. Buddy, the family dog, was very protective of her. He slept at the foot of her bed and was always close by. Mary Beth was a gentle child, talked softly, and was very compliant. She loved to pet Buddy, the family collie. She brushed him, put hair bows in his hair, and hugged him constantly. She poured her love out on Buddy, and the two had an uncommon bond.

* * * * *

Renee's phone had rung off the hook. Since Michael's death, she legally became the sole owner of his business. He owned an IT company and was a very wealthy man. Renee hired an attorney to look into the business. After carefully going over the books, they realized he had quite a few offshore accounts and gold in Switzerland. It took a whole team of accountants, but they finally discovered most of the people he had cheated. Against her attorney's advice, she returned all the monies that had been taken dishonestly. It was quite a large chunk of change, but Renee didn't care. The lawyers also found hard evidence of all the scams and dishonesty connected to the police department. Michael had bought them off in several big revenue deals. Renee didn't hesitate to blow the whistle, and it quickly made front-page news. The corrupt officers were sentenced to jail. The whole town had a collective sigh of relief. Renee hired help to sell the company as quickly as possible. She wanted nothing to do with it and wanted no reminders of Michael McCormick. She liquidated most of the accounts and put the money in the bank until she knew what to do next. It had been difficult to be across country so long. She wanted to start a new life close to Angela.

Angela had come home to help her mother get the house ready for sale. As they walked through the rooms, Renee offered for Angela to take anything she wanted.

"No, Mom." She shook her head adamantly. "I don't want anything here. Nothing. I only want you."

"Are you sure you don't want this furniture, Angela? It's new and very expensive."

"No, Mom, I don't. The only thing I wanted out of this house was you."

They looked at the mantel at the family photos, and Angela said, "Can I have these, Mom?"

"Of course, you can."

"Do you care what I do with them?"

"What do you have in mind?"

"I'd like to burn them."

They held on to each other.

"It's so surreal, Mom. I'm glad he's dead. I hate him. All these pictures make me sick."

"Your father was a sick man, honey."

"I don't want to see these pictures, and I don't want anyone else to see these lies either."

Renee nodded. They took the pictures out of the frames, and Angela struck a match to them in the fireplace.

"I hope he burns in hell forever."

"Don't, honey. Don't wish that for anyone."

Angela laid her head on her mother's shoulder and cried for all the years of pain and sorrow.

When they arrived back home, Renee handed Angela a check.

"I don't want his money, Mom."

"Don't be ridiculous, Angela. This is your inheritance. Take it. I'm taking mine gladly. He held us captive in his life. Don't let him hold us captive in his death as well."

Angela sought Godly counsel about her future. She was currently working at a bakery decorating wedding cakes. It was a rewarding job but certainly not something she wanted to do for life. After much thought and prayer, she decided to enroll in college. Her heart's desire was to be a schoolteacher. After taking several online tests and talking to several school counselors, she decided she would like to teach home economics to high school girls. She loved to cook and sew and was excited to be able to pass this along to young girls and to help prepare them for adulthood.

Renee and Angela had been going to Living Water Fellowship and had spent a great deal of time counseling with Pastor Bob and his wife, as well as Esther and some other spiritual leaders. After much soul searching, each made the difficult but life-changing decision to forgive Michael.

They had a stone ordered to mark his grave and decided to fly back to the cemetery where he was laid to rest. They laid flowers on his grave, and after taking their time talking to him through a lot of tears, they each released a white helium balloon, symbolic of letting go of the past. They stood arm in arm, looking at his name, and then walked away with a free heart, knowing the Lord had given them grace to forgive. They knew they would never return, but they were leaving with a peaceful heart. They were thankful for this closure.

Renee said, "Before we leave, I'd like to get in contact with Jonathan Avery. Without his help, none of this would have ever happened. I should have thought to get in touch with him before now."

They drove to his house, hoping he wouldn't mind them coming unannounced. She timidly knocked on his door. He answered on the first knock.

"Renee!" He said with a big smile. "It's so wonderful to see you. You look amazing! You look ten years younger!" He impulsively reached to hug her.

"This is my daughter, Angela."

He hugged Angela too.

"I can't begin to thank you, Jonathan. So much has happened, but I owe my very life to you."

"Please come in and sit," Jonathan offered.

"Oh no, we don't want to barge in."

"Not at all! I really want to talk to you." He poured them some coffee as they enjoyed sharing with him all that had transpired, even to inheriting the company and returning the funds.

"Renee, can we please keep in touch?" Jonathan asked. "I'd love to see you again."

"Yes, I'd like that. I'd like that very much."

He walked them to the car, and they hugged again.

"Mom," Angela asked, "would you be interested in seeing Jonathan?"

"I don't know, honey. I don't want to run ahead of the Lord, but I will say I'm open to anything the Lord has in store for me."

* * * * *

The following Sunday, Sharon stood in church and gave her testimony. She shared how her parents had died in an auto accident when she was young, and she had been placed in foster care. Her foster-care parents were cruel, and the foster father had sexually molested her. When she was sixteen, she stole money from him and ran as far as she could before the money ran out. She shared how Mr. Poole had found her sleeping at the park. He had been so nice to her.

He'd given her $20 a few times for food. He came one night when it was raining and offered for her to come to his home. Then how twisted he became and how he had held her captive. Then smiling, she shared about how God had sent the SWAT team to rescue her and Mary Beth. And how much her life had changed since she had asked Jesus into her heart. She felt like a brand-new person and was so in love with Jesus. She said every day she woke up grateful and full of praise and how much she loved her church family and her new family at the Belair House.

There wasn't a dry eye in the church as she ended her testimony by shyly singing her favorite hymn, "His Eye Is on the Sparrow."

Angela grabbed her mother's hand and excitedly whispered in her ear, "Mom, Jonathan's here."

Renee turned her head to look, and Jonathan was sitting on the rear pew, smiling at her. She smiled back. Renee closed her eyes and let the music flow over her as Sharon finished the song, "His eye is on the sparrow, and I know He watches me."

After church, Jonathan was waiting at the door for Renee.

She said, "Well, this is certainly a surprise. What brings you to the Shenandoah Valley?"

He said, "You. I came to speak with you."

She asked, "Is anything wrong?"

"Not at all. Will you have lunch with me?"

"Yes, of course," she said. "What is this about, Jonathan?"

He said, "It's about me wanting to court you, Renee."

She blushed and stammered.

"I'm a middle-aged man, Renee. I'm a God-fearing man. I'm a kind man, and I'd like to get to know you better."

She nodded and agreed to let him follow her home.

Waiting for their salads, Renee said, "I met Michael when I was eighteen years old. He was charming, loving, and ambitious. He was also possessive and jealous, but in my immaturity, I was flattered by it. Within a month after we were married, he started hitting me. At first, it was only once in a while, and he was always sorry. He would cry and beg me to forgive him, buy me gifts. It would be months, and he would snap over nothing and hit me again. I threatened to leave him if he ever did it again, but he slowly brainwashed and manipulated me into thinking I could never make it on my own.

"After Angela was born, I thought he would change. He loved his daughter, but he was tormented with anger. It was like a demon would overtake him at times. Although he never beat her, he was emotionally abusive to Angela but would save the beatings for me. I planned to leave him once. I had taken money out of Michael's pants pockets for several years. I never took much, just a dollar or two or some loose change. I was saving for a bus ticket to get us out of there. But he found the money I had hidden. I had it in a sock in the bottom of a box of books way back in my closet with some quilts on top of it. I didn't know he found it, but that evening, he suggested we go for a walk. I was pushing Angela in the stroller, and Roxie, our terrier, was walking with us.

"When we got to the lake, he picked up Roxie and calmly walked into the lake. He thrust her underwater. Roxie was clawing and struggling to break free. I was sobbing and begging him to let her go. He drowned my dog right in front of my eyes. With a calm voice, he said if I ever left him, that was what he would do to our daughter. I knew he meant it. My eyes were opened right then at how sick his mind was. I knew he had tapped our phone, and the risk wasn't worth it for him to harm my child.

"I was terrified of him. I had no car, no television, no books or magazines, not even a radio. Even if I could have gotten away, I didn't know where to go. He robbed me of any self-confidence. The only thing that kept me sane was my trust in God. I clung fiercely to the Lord. I never got to go to church, but I went as a child, and the few verses I learned were in my heart, and I said them over and over and over again. I wrapped my mind around God's Word, and it would settle my mind and give me peace.

"After Angela left, I had hoped to escape and be with her. I had to go to a laundromat once when my dryer was being repaired. Someone had left a small booklet. I was so desperate for anything to read that I picked it up and hid it in my laundry basket. Michael had hidden cameras everywhere to keep an eye on me, but he didn't have one in the bathroom because there was no window to escape. I used to read that book in the bathroom. It was written by a Christian evangelist, and it was about the power of the spoken word. It taught how speaking Bible verses increased your faith. I didn't know too many by heart, but the book had quite a few in there, and I read them until I memorized them, and my faith caught fire. It kept my mind sane and gave me hope. That hope kept me from giving up. I began to pray in earnest for God to make a way. Then he sent you. After living with Michael nineteen years, three months, and six days, I got away."

Jonathan had been holding her hand with both of his through the entire conversation. She looked down at their hands and looked into his eyes and smiled shyly.

"How are you doing now, Renee?"

She said, "I am well, and I am strong. Michael died of a stroke, and I no longer have to fear him. I have Jesus as my Savior. I have received a lot of emotional healing in my mind and heart. I'm sure I still have some healing that needs to take place, but Michael took so much from me, Jonathan. I'm not going to let him rob me of one more minute of my peace. I chose to forgive him, and now it's time to regain my life. I'm only forty-two years old, and I have the whole second half of my life to live."

Jonathan said, "Renee I don't want to frighten you or run ahead of God, but I want to be with you. I have so much respect for you, and I want to share my life with you. I know you are settled here with your daughter, and you've found this great church to fellowship and serve in. I'll sell my place. I have no connections there, and we'll start fresh here. I love animals and the great outdoors. I could buy a farm here on the outskirts of town. Does that appeal to you, Renee? I'd like to raise a big garden and get a dog and couple of horses. I'd like to serve the Lord with you. Grow old with me, Renee. The best is yet to be. And let's not rush it. Let me court you proper. We'll date, we'll go to the movies, we'll go for walks, we'll go out to dinner, we'll get counsel and make friends with other believers. I want you for my wife. I want to be your husband."

Renee couldn't stop the tears. He couldn't either.

"Let me be your best friend, Renee."

She nodded. He rested his forehead against hers. Words weren't necessary as they sat in the lunch booth clasping hands.

* * * * *

Isaac and Abby were on their way to Mississippi with Becca in the backseat, chatting a mile a minute

"Do Papa and Grammy have a puppy?" asked Becca.

Ever since the kidnapping, Becca had no recollection of the incident. The chloroform had erased everything from her mind except the puppy. She didn't consciously remember the dog, but she asked for a puppy continuously. Isaac had remained firm that they would not have a pet. He was gone too much to deal with an animal, and he refused to let an animal inside his home.

"Yes, love, Papa and Grammy have a dog."

Abby smiled at Isaac's exaggerated patience.

"Are we almost there?" Becca asked innocently.

At this, Abby burst out laughing. They hadn't been in the car thirty minutes. Isaac pulled over and put in a movie for Becca and put her headphones on. It was going to be long drive.

Isaac was taking Abby home to meet his family. Isaac had shared lots of stories about them, and Abby was excited to meet them. After driving for hours, they both wondered why they hadn't flown. But as they drove over the Mississippi border, Abby was glad they had taken the scenic tour. The Spanish moss was so beautiful, and the magnolia trees were gorgeous. The landscape was very different here. And Becca had been good as gold.

They passed the sign "Welcome to Jackson, Mississippi," when Isaac said, "We're almost to Grammy's, baby."

"Hurray!" cried Becca as she clapped her hands. They pulled into a big two-story colonial home with the biggest magnolia tree Abby had ever seen. They had just gotten out of the car when Isaac's parents opened the door and walked out to meet them.

"Poppy, Grammy, we're here! We're here."

Miya scooped up Becca and hugged her tight. Marion reached for her, and Becca gladly went into her arms. Marion patted her back as Becca laid her head on Marion's shoulder. Abby hung back a little to give Isaac's parents a moment of unshared joy with their granddaughter.

Becca said, "Do you have a puppy, Grammy?"

"Well, he's not exactly a puppy. He's a grown dog, but I think you two will get on fine, dear."

Isaac stepped up, pulling Abby with him. "Mom, Dad, this is Abby."

Abby felt a bit uncertain, but Marion put her arms around her and said, "I'm so glad you could come, darling. You must be simply worn to a thread from this trip. Come right in and have some refreshments."

"Hello, Mom," said Isaac.

Marion hugged him and lovingly touched his cheek. "How's my baby boy? It's so good to have you home. Miya, help Isaac with their bags."

"Not until I've hugged our Abby."

Abby smiled as Miya gave her a quick hug and kissed her cheek.

"Welcome to our home, Abby. We're so glad you could arrange your schedule to visit with us. The family will join us this evening for dinner. Everyone's looking forward to meeting you."

Marion escorted Abby into the house. The living room was large and roomy. A grandfather clock stood tall in one corner. There was a piano covered with picture frames and dozens of framed photos on the wall behind it. There was a somewhat worn but beautiful armchair that matched a sofa. The windows were high and had fabric-covered cornices that matched the sofa and chair. There was a fireplace at one end. They walked up the wide staircase with a polished banister.

"You have this room at the top of the stairs, dear." Marion opened the door, and there was a four-four poster double bed with a crocheted canopy. The wallpaper was cream with a border of tiny violets. The bed had a double-ring quilted bedspread. The wide dormer windows had tufted window seats with pillows. Everything was so lovely that it was like looking into a magazine.

"We'll have Miya place your luggage here. Now the water closet is right down the hall, dear."

Abby followed her down the hall. "How many bedrooms do you have, Mrs. Graham?" she asked.

"Please call me Marion, dear, and we have six bedrooms. This one on the left was Isaac's old room, but of course, we've changed it all now."

The room had antique mahogany furniture: a large bed, a high boy dresser, and a low writing desk opened for use. The windows had white wooden shutters. The bedspread was sage-green chenille. The hardwood floors were beautiful with a few rugs here and there, and there was an old trunk at the foot of the bed. Abby was delighted with the charm of the whole house.

"You take your time, Abby, and when you come down, we'll have some refreshments together," said Marion.

Becca was in seventh heaven petting the old Irish setter. He thumped his tail as he happily lay against Becca.

"Bootsie, you're going to have old Skipper spoiled rotten. He'll let you pet him all day long."

Becca gently patted Skipper's head as he blinked his eyes at her. She said, "Oh, Papa, this is the most beautifulest dog in the world. He has red hair, and he's so sweet."

Miya laughed and said, "He is that, my love. Skipper's a good ole fella."

They had planned dinner at six that evening. Miya was grilling chicken and corn on the cob, and the rest of the family were bringing side dishes.

"Now tell me again about the rest of the family," said Abby as they were waiting for the family to arrive.

Isaac smiled as his mother proudly said, "We have seven children. Our oldest is Carla. She married Marcus, and they have one daughter, Anne Marie. Anne Marie married and has two boys, Daniel and Aaron."

Miya laughed and said, "Let's not overwhelm her with our entire family tree, Marion. Just tell her about our seven."

"Oh yes, of course. Excuse me, dear, I just get so excited at how God has blessed our family," she said with sparkling eyes.

"Our oldest is Edmund. Then we have Carla. Thirdly is Meredith, then we have Vivian, then Genevieve, whom we call Genna, then Ava, and our baby is Isaac Alexander," she said, smiling lovingly at Isaac.

Abby was enjoying this family so much already. It was obvious how much they adored Isaac and how proud they were of his accomplishments.

Abby got up and went over to the piano and started looking at all the pictures. Marion pointed out who was who. On the wall was an enlarged wedding picture of Isaac and Rebecca. Rebecca was tall and slender with corn silk long blonde hair and crystal blue eyes. Her wedding gown was a fitted cream-colored satin. Her hair was pulled back at the sides and hung loose in the back. Isaac looked handsome in his black tux.

Abby stared at it for a moment when Marion said, "Oh, how thoughtless of me."

"Not at all," said Abby as she turned to her. "I'm not uncomfortable, Marion. The love he had for Rebecca was real and very precious. I'm secure with his love for me as well."

Marion teared as she said, "God has blessed my son twice. His cup surely overflows."

* * * * *

Andi awakened with low back pain. She waddled to the bathroom feeling achy and heavy. She had made arrangements through Social Services to place the baby for adoption. She rubbed her belly as the baby kicked hard. "I know you want out, little one." She rubbed her tummy. "I am doing this for you because I would make a terrible mother." She had grown to love the baby in spite of everything. Maternal hormones were evidently strong. She had a doctor's appointment at eleven and planned to stop at Walmart, hoping to find a pair of shorts that fit. Just as she was waddling into the store, she heard her name being called. Andi stopped and turned, and there stood her precious Mamaw. Before Andi could blink, Esther had thrown her arms around her and said, "Oh, sweet girl, my Andrea Marigold, just look at you. You're just beautiful, love. Come right over to the fountain with me and let me treat you to a cool drink."

Andi was being pulled by the hand. She wanted to resist, but the sight of her grandmother was bringing on tears. They sat down together as Mamaw wiped Andi's tears away with her ever-present hanky she had whipped out of her sleeve.

"Now just set yourself right down for a minute and let's have some iced tea. It's so good to see you, sweetheart."

Andi was mad at herself for crying. Being in Mamaw's presence almost always brought tears. Mamaw chattered on about Papaw and his garden, the strawberry patch, how she was going to make freezer jam. Andi got herself under control and just smiled at Mamaw as they drank their tea.

Andi said, "I have a doctor's appointment at eleven, Mamaw. I have to go."

"All right, sweetheart. Know that Papaw and I adore you, darling."

Andi said, "I know, Mamaw. I love you too." She waddled away as Mamaw cried into her hankie, praying fervently for her granddaughter.

"You're more than 50 percent effaced," said Dr. Jenkins at the clinic, "and three centimeters dilated. You could have this baby tonight. If you haven't gone into labor by Friday, I'm going to admit you and induce labor. You've done great with your weight. Have you been drinking alcohol?" he asked.

"No," Andi said softly.

"I'm proud of you, Andi," he said gently. "I know this hasn't been easy for you, but this will be an opportunity for you to start over."

Andi said, "Start what, Dr. Mitchell? I'm thirty years old, and I have no skills whatsoever."

He said, "Don't sell yourself short, Andi. You're a bright girl. You could go to the community college. Get a school loan and become a teacher. You could tutor on the side to earn money while you're getting your degree. Think about it." He patted her arm.

Andi struggled back into her clothing and headed for the door. Just as she got to the lobby, her water broke. She looked down at the puddle on the floor and felt a wave of panic and sorrow flood over her. She was going to give birth to her baby and give it away.

Andi was panting and sweating.

"One more push, Andi. Come on, honey, you're doing great," said the nurse.

Andi took a deep breath and pushed with all her might. The baby slipped out, and within moments, she heard her baby cry. Tears streamed into her ears. The delivery team had been informed this was an adoption and that the mother chose not to see the baby or know even if it were a boy or girl. No one said a word other than that the baby was healthy and the Apgar score was nine.

They whisked the baby away as the doctor was putting in the final stitches. The only thing Andi had requested when signing all the adoption forms was that if the baby was a girl, would the adopted parents consider giving her a middle name of a flower? When the social worker read that request, she looked up at Andi and said, "I'm sure there's a story here. Care to share?"

Andi looked at her with sad eyes and said, "Four generations of girls in my family have been named after flowers. My great mother had five daughters. She named them Daisy, Lilly, Violet, Rose, and Iris. My grandmother was Esther Rose. She had two daughters named Ivy and Holly. My mother was Helene Ivy, and she had identical twin daughters. My name is Andrea Marigold, and my sister's is Abigail."

"What's Abigail's middle name?"

Andi laughed and said, "She swore me to secrecy. She hates it so much that she said no one would ever know it except her husband."

The social worker smiled and said, "I'll pass on your request."

Andi thanked her, trying not to cry again.

Three days later, Andi felt desolate as her breasts throbbed full of milk. She felt alone and futile. Suddenly a verse Mamaw made her memorize flashed through her mind:

> I will never leave thee nor forsake thee.
> (Hebrews 13:5)

Andi felt strangely comforted as she drifted off into much-needed sleep.

* * * * *

The hospital social worker had befriended Andi and suggested she hook up with AA. Although she had refrained from drinking during her pregnancy, Andi knew she was an alcoholic and knew she would slip again, especially in light of depression settling over her. Andi looked through the yellow pages and found several listings. She made some calls and decided to attend a meeting. She wanted to start her life in a new direction, and maybe they could offer her something to help.

Andi had been attending the meetings for several months and had made a few acquaintances. The meetings were sort of like church without the guilt and pressure. At least these people knew how it felt to want a drink, and she didn't get judged for it. There were a few do-gooders who wanted to pound the Bible down her throat, and some wanted to get a little too close. Andi kept her guard up, but she kept going. The 12-step program really was helpful. All the letters she wrote helped ease her conscience, but she still felt lonely and unsettled.

Andi was scanning the help wanted ads when she saw a listing for Morning Side Assisted Living Facility. They needed help for the night shift. She wasn't a certified nursing assistant, but she was going to apply and see what happened.

She received a tour of the facility from the owner.

"This position does not require you to be a state licensed CNA, Andi. Your duties will be to check each patient every hour, change their briefs every three hours, and there is a list of nightly chores divided between the employees."

The work was full-time with benefits. Andi was blown away at the pay. She could quit waitressing and get a student loan to go to school full-time. She could grab sleep in the evenings before her midnight shift started. This was perfect for her. Andi had taken a hard look at her life and knew at her age something had to give. She was going to bite the bullet and return to school. She had known she had a gift to teach since she was a child. *Better late than never*, she thought. She signed the employment contract with a happy heart and thanked her new employer. Andi knew that the only reason she got the job was because she had used Abby as a reference. Everyone in the area knew and respected her sister, but that was fine. Andi wanted a fresh start, and this was her beginning step.

Two months later, she was on duty when she found Miss Mazie covering up the patients again.

"Now, Miss Mazie, you're going to get me fired. They'll get rid of me if you don't quit doing my job."

Miss Mazie had her nights and days mixed up. She would nap during the day and walk the halls or play the piano at night. Mazie McIntyre turned to her and pointed her finger in her face and began to prophesy. Andi had never seen her do this before, and it made the hair stand up on the back of her neck.

"Thus sayeth the Lord of Hosts, I have called thee by name, My daughter. I have placed within you gifts, and I will cause those gifts to come forth. You will teach with authority and with an anointing, says the Lord. Run to Me, and I will set your feet in a high place and give you peace of mind and favor. Search for Me with all your heart, and you will find me, for I have loved you with an everlasting love."

Miss Mazie walked off and left Andi shaking from head to toe. Ordinarily, the nurses laughed and shared what Miss Mazie said, but Andi didn't feel like laughing. She felt like she was standing on holy ground. She went into the bathroom and leaned her head against the wall. *God, was that really You talking through Miss Mazie? Do You really love me? I'm a bad person, God. But I'm sure You know all about that.* Andi started to leave, but she felt the presence of the Lord flow over her like warm honey. Instead of feeling guilt and fear, she felt intense love. She slid down the wall and wrapped her arms around her knees. She bowed her head but didn't know what to say. *I'm sorry I killed my babies.* The bitter tears fell from her eyes. *I'm so sorry. Please, God, forgive me. I'm sorry for how screwed up my life is. I'm sorry for all the mistakes I've made. Help me, Jesus. I believe in You. How could I not? Please forgive me. Show me the way, Lord. I can't go on like this. I need You.*

Peace coursed through her being as she felt weighed to the floor. *Please watch over my child, Lord. Please let my baby's parents love him and keep him safe. And please help me get my life straightened out. Thank You, God. Thank You.* She got up feeling light, and a strange sense of joy washed over her. It felt foreign not to feel the heavy weight of guilt. She washed her face and stepped into the hall, and a song her parents had taught her and Abby as very young children came to mind. "If you're happy and you know it, clap your hands." Andi smiled and softly clapped her hands as she went to check her next patient.

* * * * *

Becca jumped on Isaac's bed at daybreak.

"Daaaddy, today's the day. Get up, get up! We're getting married today."

He laughed as she jumped up and down on the bed.

The wedding was to take place at the Shenandoah River. The river had been their refuge in times of trouble, sadness, vacation, and solace. It seemed only fitting to hold their wedding ceremony there as well. A family friend had given them permission to hold the wedding on his property. He had five beautiful acres that backed up to the river. White wooden folding chairs had been set up in the grass by the riverbank. A beautiful iron arch had been erected and was covered with wisteria. They had chosen not to have a traditional wedding, much to everyone's surprise. Even though Abby had waited so long to be married, it was the marriage she had waited for, not the wedding ceremony. Abby and Isaac had both agreed they wanted it simple but meaningful. Isaac's parents had flown in. Abby's parents and grandparents were in attendance, as well as Andi and a few of their closest friends. Becca was not going to be the flower girl. Instead, she was going to quote scripture. Abby and Isaac had worked with her, and Becca was excited to share.

Pastor Bob from Living Water was officiating the ceremony. Little Donnie's whole family were in attendance. The entire family played stringed instruments. They were playing the bull bass, twelve-string acoustic guitar, banjo, dobro, steel guitar, violin, and little Donnie was playing the autoharp. The whole family were musical geniuses. The children could play before they started school.

When they started playing the wedding march, Becca walked down the aisle between the chairs, smiling shyly at everyone. She was wearing a bright-yellow sleeveless dress, white ruffled socks, and black patent leather Mary Janes. She had a daisy flower ring in her hair.

Isaac and Abby walked down side by side. Isaac had on black slacks and a crisp white shirt. Abby wore a black-and-white sleeveless dress with a long silver necklace and black-and-white bracelets.

As they were walking down, Isaac whispered in Abby's ear, "What's your middle name, Abigail?"

Abby smiled and said, "We're not married yet!"

They stood under the arch covered with wisteria with the Shenandoah River for a backdrop. Donnie's family continued to play hymns softly as they recited their vows.

When it was Becca's turn, she spoke in a clear voice, "Genesis 2:18: "And the Lord God said, 'It is not good that man should be alone. I will make him a helper.' Psalms 113:9: 'He maketh the barren woman to keep house, and to be a joyful mother of children.' God sent Abby to be a wife to my daddy and a mommy to me."

Becca beamed at everyone as she stepped back, relieved of her duty.

Donnie eased up beside Isaac, carrying his autoharp.

Isaac said, "I wrote a song that I'd like to share. This song was birthed in prayer, and it expresses both my heart and Abby's."

Abby was surprised as she didn't know Isaac had written this.

> There is a river that flows from your throne
> There is a river that flows from your throne
> For your glory, let it flow through me I am
> your laborer
> Here, I am send me
>
> There is a river
> The river of God is deep and wide
> Won't you step in and with Him abide
> Let the living water flow over your soul
> The power of His blood will make you whole.

The sweet music floated on the breeze down the river. When the song was finished, Pastor Bob said, "I now pronounce you man and wife."

Everyone clapped as Isaac and Abby kissed.

Andi hugged Abby and said, "I'm so proud for you, sis. You look beautiful."

Abby said, "I'm really proud of you too, Andi."

Andi stood back and watched everyone as they hugged and laughed. Abby's parents had rented a blue-and-white striped tent and local caterers who had started the pig roast at dawn. They gathered to enjoy a sumptuous meal of pulled pork with all the fixings. Mamaw Esther made the wedding cake. It was her famous homemade coconut cake. Andi had found an adorable top for the cake. It was a doctor and nurse kissing.

After dinner, no one was in a hurry to leave. The weather was perfect, and everyone was enjoying fellowship. Andi walked over to the river and picked up a rock.

Her grandfather walked up behind her and said, "In the mood for company?"

She smiled as he handed her a flat rock, and they skipped their rocks together.

"How's the tutoring going, shug?"

Andi smiled and said, "It's going great, Papaw."

"How many kids you tutoring at present?"

"Just two for now. One little boy, age eleven. We're doing fractions. And one fourteen-year-old I'm tutoring in reading. He's got dyslexia, and I've found a great tool that you lay down over each word. It helps your brain see the letters in order. It's not only improved his grades, it's improved his attitude."

Papaw laughed and said, "It's improved yours too, kiddo." He put his arm around her, and they walked back. "Are your classes going well?" he asked.

"Yes, sir, they really are. I'll be getting my teaching certificate soon."

"Your grandmother and I are so proud of you, Andi."

She kissed his cheek and said, "I know you are, Papaw. I love you so."

"Of course, you do." Papaw laughed. "I let you win at checkers."

* * * * *

Isaac slowly opened his eyes. Abby was asleep with her head on his chest. He put his arms around her and rubbed her back. Her skin was so smooth and soft. She cuddled a little closer. The sounds of the waves were lulling them back to sleep when Isaac said, "Hey, Mrs. Graham. I think it's high time you told me your middle name."

Abby said, "Oh, Isaac, I was hoping you'd forget about that."

"Ha, not on your life."

She laughed and said, "Okay, brace yourself. It's Zinnia."

"Really? Like the flower?"

"Yep. Wow, I would have never guessed that in a million years."

"I'm sure."

"Is there a story here?"

"In my family line, four generations deep, all the women were given names of flowers."

"What about Mamaw Esther?"

"Her name is Esther Rose."

"What about your mom?"

"Her name is Helene Ivy."

"How about Andi?"

"Andrea Marigold."

Isaac laughed and said, "That's incredible, Abigail Zinnia."

Abby got up and put her robe on.

"Do you think Becca will be okay without us for a whole week?"

"Absolutely. Your parents will spoil her rotten."

"Want to join me for a swim?" he asked.

"No, you go ahead. I'll come down in a bit."

Isaac walked down to the shore and waded in. Abby lay back on the bed and stretched. It was hard to believe they had been on their honeymoon for five days. The weather had been perfect. She'd never been to Jamaica. The island was small, only eleven miles long, and they had toured, hiked, rented mopeds, and taken tons of snapshots of the beautiful lush foliage. They had their photos taken wearing flower leis and had bought some wonderful gifts for Becca and her family.

* * * * *

Andi was making her nightly rounds at Morning Star. She was surprised Miss Mazie wasn't walking about getting underfoot. Maybe she's finally gotten her night and days straightened out, thought Andi. She eased open Miss Mazie's door and went to check on her. She was curled up on her side looking so at peace. Andi hated to disturb her, but she needed to check to see if she was dry. When she turned back the blanket, she realized sweet Miss Mazie had gone to be with Jesus.

Word spread through town like wildfire about Miss Mazie's passing. They held her home-going celebration in the high school auditorium. It was the largest gathering place in town. Tables were weighed down with food. It seemed the whole town had come out to pay their last respects. Becca sang "Great Is Thy Faithfulness," Miss Mazie's favorite hymn. Pastor Bob preached a wonderful message truly celebrating her life well lived. The platform was banked in flowers, and they dressed Miss Mazie in an elegant petal-pink suit with matching gloves and a pale-pink hat. When they laid her body to rest at Willow Green Cemetery, a dozen white doves were released. They circled and flew off.

Mrs. Anderson was making a menu for the next week's meals when Victoria walked into the kitchen.

"Here, dear, I finished up Monday to Friday's evening meals. I was thinking we might do something special for the weekend. Since the weather is so warm, why don't we grill out?"

"And Sunday, how about a nice beef roast? The meat can roast while we work on the dessert. I was thinking apple cobbler would do nicely. And to go with it, we'll make homemade ice cream. I found an ice-cream maker in the pantry, and it works perfectly. I have a wonderful recipe. We just need rock salt."

"Mrs. Anderson, you already spoil our boarders rotten."

"Well, dear, we're the only family they have. And they're the only family we have," she said, smiling happily.

After deciding to turn her inherited house into a boarding-house, Victoria went to visit Mrs. Anderson in the nursing home. Her stroke had been mild, but her daughter and son-in-law made it clear they didn't want to be burdened by taking care of her. Victoria told Mrs. Anderson about her inheritance with great enthusiasm.

"I need your help. I feel so inadequate."

"I can't imagine how I could be of help, dear, but I'm certainly happy for you, and I have great confidence in you. You are a bright girl, and you can be successful at anything you put your mind to."

"Mrs. Anderson, I have no family. You're my only family. Please come home with me. My house is huge, and I need your support."

"No, dear. I appreciate what you're saying, but my body has been weakened from the stroke, and I would only be a burden to you."

"Nonsense," said Victoria sharply. "Your muscles and coordination may have been slightly affected, but your mind and heart certainly aren't." Victoria knelt down at Mrs. Anderson's chair. "I love you, and I need you. We need each other. Please live with me. My boarders will need a mother figure. I trust you, and I need your experience and friendship."

Victoria's tears were dripping off her chin. She looked Mrs. Anderson in the eyes and said, "You don't want to live here. Let's leave right now. I'm sorry your family put you here. It's ludicrous, outrageous. But it's their loss and my gain. I'm not leaving here without you. You're my best friend. I've prayed about this—oh, how I've prayed. I know the Lord wants us to be together forever. I know He does."

Mrs. Anderson buried her face in her hands and wept. Victoria laid her head on her lap and cried with her.

"Look at us." Mrs. Anderson laughed. "We're a mess."

Victoria said, "If you don't say yes, you'll break my heart."

Mrs. Anderson put both hands on Victoria's face and said, "You've convinced me. Let's pack my things and vacate the premises. We have work to do."

Victoria hugged her tightly as they laughed.

Mrs. Anderson said, "I feel like I'm dreaming."

Victoria said, "Me too! Come on, we've got a boardinghouse to run. We need to paint and paper and decorate—and wait until you see this place! It is absolutely amazing. Aunt Mazie had really eclectic taste. Every room is like a treasure trove. But what about your son and family? Will they be upset?"

Mrs. Anderson said, "I'll call them and let them know later. I am in charge of my own affairs, and they have no control over me. They were quite upset with me when I refused to sign for them to become my power of attorney. But in the end, they will see it is all for the best."

They continued chatting as they quickly packed Mrs. Anderson's belongings and headed *home*.

Together they planned and prayed and remodeled. Mrs. Anderson has been a plethora of knowledge and wisdom. She helped Victoria make wise decisions with her finances. It took months to complete and was finally time to advertise for boarders. They had filled the rooms within six weeks. Victoria was shocked at how many people applied. It had been difficult to decide which ones to accept. She wanted to take them all, but she and Mrs. Anderson went over each application carefully, calling references, praying, and finally decided on two men and two women.

* * * * *

Laurie and Dale laughed as their daughter scooted across the carpet. She couldn't walk, but she could crawl as fast as lightning. Laurie watched her husband lay on the floor and block Lexus from the toy she wanted. Lexus sat back and giggled and crawled over top of his body to get to her bear. It was still hard to believe they were parents. After the birth mother changed her mind and decided to keep her baby, Laurie was so devastated that she vowed to never put herself through that again.

But just ten weeks later, Pastor Koby came over and said, "I have another baby for you, Laurie."

Dale had to convince her to open her heart, and she was so glad she did. Lexus was the joy of their life. They brought her home when she was five days old. She had dark curly hair and a huge smile with deep dimples. Unless she was wet or hungry, Lexus was always happy. They had planned to adopt two more children over the next several years.

Laurie and Dale's church was the center focus of their life. The pastor had a true shepherd's heart. He was involved in the lives of his congregation. The worship team was awesome, and they had ministry opportunities for all ages. They had a single's group, a grief recovery group, an archery club, a bowling league, softball league, and a motorcycle club. Anytime anyone had an interest and offered to step up to the plate, another ministry was born. They had home cell groups, in-depth Bible studies, financial classes, parenting classes. The list was endless.

Laurie and Dale had grown so much in their spiritual walk. Laurie was a Sunday school teacher, and Dale was an usher, a Royal Ranger leader, and a member of the motorcycle gang called the Christian Cruisers.

Lexus was just turning five years old, and Dale had finally convinced Laurie to start riding on his Harley with him. The Cruisers were going for a ride to Oakley, a town about an hour away to a seafood restaurant. All the wives were riding on the back with their spouses. They had gotten five senior high school girls to watch all the kids at church while they were gone. The kids were going to have a ball watching movies, popping popcorn, and playing games.

Laurie and Dale never saw it coming. The young driver ran the red light at eighty miles per hour and hit them broadside. Laurie flew up in the air and landed flat on her back on the highway. Dale had been knocked off and dragged. Laurie was killed instantly. Dale had two broken legs, a broken pelvis, four cracked ribs, and a punctured kidney. The Cruisers were in a state of shock as they stood helplessly sobbing in the highway.

The driver was a teen who had just gotten his driver's license. He had argued with his mother and taken off like a bat out of a high pine, driving like a maniac. The boy was unhurt physically, but marred for life emotionally. Someone had called his parents as he stared in horror at the broken bodies on the road. His parents drove onto the scene and ran to their son. As soon as he saw his mother, he fell to his knees, weeping with inconsolable, harsh sobs. His parents were in shock, trying to comfort their son and overwhelmed with sorrow for the senseless death of this young wife and mother and the severe injury of the father. The rescue squads and fire trucks came blaring in as everyone continued crying and walking around in a daze.

They postponed the funeral until Dale got out of the hospital. His friends rolled his wheelchair into the church. The service was a blur. Dale was on painkillers and fell asleep before it was over. A very somber crowd drove to the cemetery to lay Laurie's body to rest. Friends and family filed by, not knowing what to say. The people tried to say a few words to Dale, but he never acknowledged anyone.

Laurie's mother took Lexus home with her for a month. Dale didn't argue. He slept on the couch most of the time and became more depressed and bitter. His body finally began to heal, but his spirit was still bleeding.

Dale started having a drink at bedtime. It made him sleep better. But soon it increased to two. After that, it escalated. He never drank at work, but as soon as he came home, it started. He dropped a bomb on his parents when he told them he was selling his home and relocating. They did their level best to talk him out of it.

"Where will you go? How will you care for Lexus without help? Why are you moving away from us?"

Dale said if he lived in the house any longer, he'd lose his mind.

"Laurie is everywhere. I can't sleep in my own bed. I see her everywhere, and I need a fresh start."

His mother said, "But what about Lexus? She starts school this year. And where will you go to church?"

Dale stiffened at hearing about church. He was mad at God for taking his wife. "We'll be fine. I'll be in touch."

Amidst everyone's pleading, he hired a moving company to pack him out. His house had been on the market five days when he got a contract. He had been looking at real estate on the internet, and he had met some new friends who told him about a place in the Shenandoah Valley area. With Lexus in tow, he moved the following weekend.

They found a beautiful home in Hillcrest Heights. His house was about 1,800 square feet, all on one floor. His lot was one full acre and sat at the end of cul-de-sac. It was a safe place for Lexus to ride her bike. He was working from home via computer, fax, and phone, but he was lonely and sick of being depressed. He found a Christian school with before and after care for Lexus. They settled in a routine of sorts. They got up, ate breakfast, he brushed her hair, dressed her, and dropped her at day care. He came home and worked, picked her up by three, and she played with the neighbor kids, rode her bike. They fixed dinner, she had her bath and story time, and was in bed by eight o'clock. Once she was asleep Dale poured himself a drink or two or three and watched TV till he passed out.

* * * * *

Abby's cell phone rang while she was watering the garden. She had the phone in her pocket.

"Abby?"

"Hi, Andi, what are you up to?" Abby looked over to see Becca running back and forth under the sprinkler.

"I have some fun news. Or shall I say a fun invitation for you guys."

"Oh yeah, what's going on?"

"Mamaw and Papaw have invited Mom and Dad, you, Isaac, and Becca and me to their place for a weekend camping trip by the creek."

"What? Are you kidding me?"

"No, really. Mamaw and Papaw said they were lonely and wanted to do a bonfire, a fish fry, the whole deal."

"When?"

"This weekend. They have Isaac's rotation schedule and knew he was off this weekend."

"Sounds great to me. Let me talk to him, and I'll get back to you."

Abby was excited and hoped Isaac would be willing. She remembered so many wonderful times of fellowship camping with her parents. She could hardly wait till Isaac got home from work.

"Honey, this sounds more like work than fun."

"Oh, Isaac, don't rain on my parade. Say you'll come, please?"

She looked so pitiful that he said, "Okay, I'm in."

"Great, we'll have such fun, you'll see."

Isaac rolled his eyes as he looked back at the family. He helped Papaw and Mark haul the tents, the propane cookstove, all the cooking pots, utensils, groceries, sleeping bags, floats, blankets, and chairs. If all he had to do was lie on a raft in the river and eat fresh fried fish, he'd have a blast too. But he couldn't help but smile as he heard them shouting with laughter. Andi was in the river with Becca, teaching her how to float. Becca had floaters on her arms and a float swimsuit. She would float even if she didn't try. They had caught dozens of bluegill, and Papaw had gone to the trouble to filet them no matter what size they were. Isaac was getting a lesson in mixing spices and egg batter. They smelled heavenly as they were frying. Later that evening, they had planned a bonfire, roasting marshmallows, and catching fireflies in a jar. Isaac was thankful the gnats and mosquitoes were somewhat at bay.

Papaw had sewn himself a gnat hat. He looked a bit ridiculous, like a lopsided beekeeper in his goofy mesh hat, long sleeves, and long pants. Everyone else had on shorts and tank tops.

He said, "Go ahead and laugh. I don't care what I look like. I'm not getting sunburned or bug bitten."

It was dusk, and they were roasting marshmallows when Abby said, "Tell us some stories, Papaw."

They all agreed, and everyone got comfortable as Papaw began to tell about his childhood. Although they'd all heard these stories over the years, they still loved for him to share.

"Of course, we never had any real toys. When I was about seven years old. I remember running the creek bed looking for the perfect rocks. It might take me four or five days to find and collect just the right ones. Only the smooth rocks would do. I wanted white ones and black ones because they were my cows. I had a herd of over a hundred cows. I then collected sticks. I cut them exactly two inches tall and stuck them in the ground one inch apart. I spent days into weeks collecting the sticks and cutting them with a sharp rock or broken pieces of glass so they were all the same size. The sticks were my fenced corrals. I played in the dirt for hours moving the cows one at a time from corral to corral. And of course, I had the wildest stallion in the land. Mama would save me her old broomstick and the cotton string from the flour sacks. I found an old piece of broken glass that I used to cut a slit in the side of the stick. I shredded the cotton string and wedged it in that slit to be the horse's mane. I had a couple of strips of rubber from an old inner tube as my bridle. I could fly like the wind. My stallion would rear up, and I'd jump around and shout, 'Ho there!' I rode that horse till the back of the stick was worn to a point."

Everyone laughed as they could imagine their precious grandfather running barefoot riding that stick horse.

Lying on the sleeping bag looking at the stars, they all lay softly chatting when Mamaw started singing clear and high. Soon everyone joined in. Andi hadn't thought of that song in years and years.

"There are some things I may not know. There are some places I cannot go. But there's one thing, of this I'm sure. My God is real, for I can feel Him in my soul. My God is real, real in my soul. My God is real, for He has cleansed and made me whole. His love for me is like pure gold. My God is real, for I can feel Him in my soul."

There was no need for more talk after the song ended. Everyone drifted off into sweet slumber to the gentle sound of the flowing river.

The smell of hot coffee and sizzling bacon wafted on the breeze.

"Mamaw must have gotten up before daylight," said Abby as she rolled out of her sleeping bag. "Come on, sleepyhead, or there won't be any food left."

Isaac groaned as he tried to stretch the kinks out of his back. He had slept very little, between the hard ground and scratching bug bites. Becca was "helping" Mamaw Esther set the table for breakfast. Everyone gathered around as they said the blessing.

"I guess carrying all those pots and pans and stove and groceries was worth it after all," Isaac said, laughing.

There were scrambled eggs with cheese in black iron skillets, bacon fried to perfection, fried potatoes with onion, sausage gravy over bread, orange juice, and coffee. Everyone ate heartily and relished the cool morning temperatures. There was no humidity, and everyone lingered after the meal. Papaw read scripture, and everyone prayed together. Helen was a great organizer and gave everyone a job; and in short order, things were cleaned, packed up, and ready to roll.

Esther said, "Now, before everyone leaves, Thomas and I have something we'd like to share with you."

Thomas stood up and said, "You all know I have thirty-five acres on the farm. We have decided to donate ten acres to start a Community Christian Camp for the youth in this and the surrounding areas. We decided on the tract that includes the lake. We thought it best not to have river frontage for safety purposes. We have already drawn up the papers with our attorney. And we have asked Jonathan and Renee Avery to manage it for us. This will not be a nonprofit camp. There will be a fee, and we believe it will be quite a profitable business. We will accept registrations from churches for campers and will be open June, July, and August. We will build cabins furnished with bunks, a rec hall, a chapel, and a swimming pool. We have already talked with many business owners who have agreed in writing to donate monthly funds as well as immediate funds for expenses such as zip lines, paint ball, and such. We foresee horseback riding and also weeks for special needs children. We have had promises of paddleboats, canoes, and safety-jacket donations from the Sports Aquarium. We foresee it being ready in ten months, and we hope we have your support."

Everyone was laughing and talking over top of one another with excitement.

Abby said, "I'll take a week off my vacation to be a camp counselor."

Isaac said, "*Amen.* Great idea. I will too."

Andi said, "Count me in."

It took over an hour for everyone to settle down and pack up.

"We should do this again," said Mamaw.

Everyone excitedly agreed that it would be an annual tradition to have a campout weekend together. "By then, we can use the new camp. We'll reserve a time just for the family every year."

* * * * *

Andi looked out the window at the snow and smiled. She loved snowy days. No school today. She turned on the radio, and sure enough, the announcer was saying no school. She knew her students would be thrilled as she had been as a kid. She cuddled under the quilt and decided to try to get a little more sleep.

* * * * *

"Daddy, Daddy, look out the window. Daddy, wake up," said Lexus excitedly.

"What is it, Kit?" said Dale in a gravelly voice.

"It's snowing," she shouted into his face. Lexus had never seen snow, and she was very excited to get out in it and play. "Can we make a snowman, Dad? And a snow fort? And have a snowball fight? Can we, Daddy, please? Get up, Dad."

Dale laughed even though he had a hangover. "All right, Kit Kat, go on out and let me get dressed. We'll get some breakfast and find you some warm clothes."

"Goody, goody," she yelled, clapping her hands.

Dale heard her feet pounding down the hall. He went into the bathroom and looked at himself in the mirror. He looked rough and felt worse. He turned on the shower and stepped in. He leaned against the wall, letting the hot water course over him. The steam helped his headache a little, but he needed a drink to get his head to stop pounding. The ever-present guilt settled over him as he got dressed.

I need help, he said as he tied his boots. *I need to get back to my AA meetings. I haven't been in three weeks. If I'm going to be a decent father to Lexus, I need to get my life together.* He looked around with disgust at his filthy house. *I'll hire a housekeeper while I'm at it. I'm sick of this mess.*

Christmas was sixteen days away, and he hadn't even shopped. He had to get his act together. He went to Lexus's bedroom to search for warm clothes. He felt ashamed as he looked around. Laurie would be heartbroken to see what his life had come to. Lexus's bedroom was in shambles. Clothes and toys and bedding tumbled every which way. He started routing through her things and realized she didn't have proper winter clothes. He was shocked at how he had neglected her needs. He ended up putting several pairs of socks on her and a couple of sweat suits over top of each other with her coat and gloves and one of his hats. He would take care of her winter clothing that very day. He wasn't even sure what size she needed.

Lexus's lips were blue as she begged not to go in. "Not yet, Daddy, this is so fun."

He said, "You're going to turn into a snowman, Lexie."

"A snowman?!" she squealed with delight. "Daddy, I'm a girl."

He smiled sadly as he thought how much Laurie would love to see her face flushed with excitement all covered with snow. "Your daddy's freezing. Let's go in and get warmed up."

He drew a bath for her and settled her in the tub.

"Daddy, can we get a Christmas tree?"

He said, "We'll see."

She said, "Can we get one today?"

"We'll see."

"Daaad."

"Take your bath. I'll go find you something to put on."

Dale rummaged through her clothes again, shocked that he'd been blinded to the condition of his home. Not only was her room, but the whole house in shambles. He decided to go shopping right after lunch. No, they'd eat out today.

* * * * *

Andi had been sober for four years and seven months. AA had been so helpful to her. And once she had given her heart to Jesus, her whole life changed. She had been able to finish her degree and was teaching school. She had started with kindergarten but had taught third grade for the last two years. God had been so good to her to give her a fresh start. She felt led to still be involved in AA. She was a gifted counselor, and they usually gave her the snarly people. Andi knew how it felt, and their prickly exterior did not intimidate her. Andi had been assigned to Dale, but she had her work cut out for her. He acted like a bear with a sore paw. She wasn't fooled by his smart-mouth remarks. She knew he was reaching out, but he wanted to get a rise out of her. But he hadn't bargained for Andi Alexander.

The phone rang as he was headed out the door.

"Hello?" Dale said a bit gruffly.

"Dale? This is Andi Alexander."

Dale wasn't in the mood to hear from his AA sponsor, especially since he'd just guzzled a beer, but if he was going to brave the Christmas madness, he needed something to calm his nerves.

"How are you, Dale?"

"I'm doing just great. Couldn't be better," he said sarcastically.

Andi laughed and said, "What's going on?"

He said, "I'm taking my kid shopping for clothes, and it's not my favorite thing."

"You have a child? You never mentioned that before."

"Yeah, well, I do."

"A girl or boy?"

"A girl. She's five."

"That's great, Dale. Where are you going shopping?"

"Oh man, I don't know. The mall, I guess."

Andi laughed and said, "I take it you're not a shopper."

"That's an understatement," he said. "I'm not sure what size she wears. She needs everything. It makes me feel kind of sick to think about it."

Andi felt compassion for him and concern that the pressure might make him make some bad choices. "Do you need some help, Dale?"

"What do you mean?"

"I mean…do you want me to go with you and help shop for your daughter?"

Dale felt rescued and jumped at the opportunity. "Yes, Andi, I would. I'll pay you."

"Don't be ridiculous. It'd be my pleasure. Are you leaving now?"

"Yes, we're on our way out the door."

"Okay, I'll meet you in front of JCPenney in thirty minutes. When I say the front, I mean inside the mall. Do you know where I mean? It's right beside the bookstore."

"I'll find it, and thanks, Andi. Really, this means a lot."

Andi shook her head as she looked at the papers she was going to grade. *Oh well, this is more important.* She went down the hall to dress and tried to think what his child would need.

Andi was waiting in front of Penney's when she saw Dale walking down holding the hand of a beautiful little girl. She had on mismatched clothes that had seen better days, and her hair needed to be washed. She was obviously enjoying the Christmas decorations chattering constantly. Dale looked miserable but at least seemed to be showing patience toward his daughter. Dale smiled when he spotted her and said, "Thanks again, Andi."

Andi said, "Sure, it'll be fun."

Dale stooped down and said, "Lexus, this is Ms. Alexander. Can you say hi?"

"Hello, Lexus, it's nice to meet you," Andi said, "You have a beautiful little girl. She doesn't look like you, does she?"

Dale laughed and said, "Lucky her."

Lexus was oblivious and happily took Andi's hand as they headed for the children's department. Andi systematically started looking through the department. "What's your budget today, Dale?" she asked.

Dale said, "It doesn't matter. I want to get her what she needs and be done with it."

"What does she need?" asked Andi.

"Literally everything. She doesn't have hardly any clothes that fit."

"Okay, let's get started."

They tried some things on to gauge her size, and Dale walked along carrying armloads.

Dale was really impressed with Andi's shopping ability and especially her speed. After only an hour and twenty minutes, they had purchased underpants, socks, T-shirts, pajamas, four pants-and-shirt outfits, two new sweatsuits, some warm turtlenecks, two cute pullover sweaters, a winter coat, gloves, a hat, two new dresses, tights, a pair of sneakers, a pair of patent leather shoes, snow boots, and bedroom slippers with monkeys on them. Lexus had fallen in love with Andi and was reluctant to leave her. Dale realized for the first time how much she needed female influence.

They were all starving and decided to walk down to the food court to grab something to eat. Dale went to order as Andi and Lexus waited at the table.

"How old are you Lexus?"

"I'm five."

"When's your birthday?"

"August 12."

Andi couldn't help but think about her own child. Her child would have been five this year too on August 7, but she didn't know if she'd had a girl or boy. As Lexie sat chattering, Andi was looking at her big brown eyes and dark curly hair. She kept staring at her when it suddenly dawned on her that this little face reminded her of a photo she had of her mother, Helen.

Dale walked over with their lunch, and Andi asked if she could pray over their lunch. Dale said sure, and Andi bowed her head and prayed. The conversation was easy as they sat eating together.

"I need a housekeeper," said Dale. "Would you know of anyone?"

Andi asked, "How often do you want someone to come?"

Dale said, "I don't know. What's normal?"

Andi laughed and realized how helpless this man was. She knew his wife had been killed in a tragic motorcycle accident but knew nothing else. "You'd probably need someone to come in and clean it really well the first time. It may even take more than a day, but then probably every two weeks would be sufficient."

Dale nodded and asked, "Do you know much I should pay?"

Andi said, "How big is your house?"

"It's an 1,800 square foot one-story."

Andi thought a moment and said, "You'll probably be paying around $200 per cleaning, and it will be more the first time. How bad is it?"

Dale cut his eyes at her and said. "It's bad."

Andi had been needing some extra money for Christmas and impulsively said, "I'll do it, Dale."

Dale snapped his head up and said, "Why?"

"Because I need the money. I need to buy Christmas presents and pay my taxes. My teacher's salary isn't bad, but I could use some extra right now. I was just praying for God to provide me opportunities to make some extra money."

Dale said, "I never thought of myself as an answer to prayer, but when can you start?"

She laughed and said, "Why not today?"

Dale was embarrassed and said, "No, no, I need to clear it up a bit first."

Andi said, "Then we'll work together. Let's just get it over with. Do you have any cleaning supplies?"

Dale looked lost and said, "Uh, like what?"

Andi laughed and said, "I'll take care of it."

Andi was impressed with the outside of his home. It was a nice neighborhood. But when she walked in the door, it was all she could do not to react. Her compassion was so great for this man and his daughter. The neglect was rampant. She said, "Let's have a walk through and decide what to do first."

He showed her around, looking embarrassed.

"I have an idea," she told Dale. "Why don't you go all over the house and gather up all the trash. Take a trash bag with you and empty all the trash cans and go through each room and anything you can throw away, do it."

Andi had noticed there were pizza boxes, soda cans, Chinese takeout cartons, and a host of other trash all over the house. Andi said, "I'm going to start in Lexus's room. Okay, Lex, you can be my helper."

Andi went to her closet and took almost all the clothing out as she saw it was too small for her. She folded it and put it in bags by the door to be donated. Then she took out all the new clothes, removed the tags, and hung them up. Next she cleaned out the dresser drawers and threw out and sorted and, in short order, had everything folded neatly in the drawers. Next she cleared off the top of the dressers, dusting and sorting as she went. "Let's go through your toys, Lexus. Let's get rid of all the broken ones and all the ones you don't play with anymore." That took a little coaxing, but soon Andi had good order with the toys.

She then attacked the bookshelf. She dumped everything out in the floor and sat down cross-legged to sort, but before she could blink, Lexus jumped in her lap and begged her to read her a story. Andi wrapped her arms around her in a tight hug and said, "I promise I'll read to you when we're finished." It took forty-five minutes to sort and stack her books. She took the sheets off the bed and went to the laundry room. "Where are the clean sheets?" she called to Dale.

Dale had done a credible job of sorting through the living room and kitchen. There were already three huge bags of trash. He said, "We don't have an extra set, just one for each bed."

Andi said, "Let's start you a shopping list."

Dale went to find a pen and paper, and Andi said, "Let's get two extra sets of sheets for her bed and one extra for yours. And if money's not a problem, let's get her a new bedspread and curtains."

Dale suddenly remembered Laurie's mother crying when she came to visit and wanted to fix up Lexus's room. Dale had been drinking, and his mother-in-law's offer made him feel guilty, like he wasn't taking care of his child, so he told her to get out.

Dale's self-hatred was suffocating at times. Andi misunderstood his look and quickly said, "Hey, no problem, Dale. I get carried away at times."

"No, she does need new bedding. I was just thinking about my mother-in-law and her offering to help. I was drinking at the time."

Andi said, "Say no more. Believe me, if I had a dollar for every time I offended my family, I would be rich."

Dale was grateful that she really did understand. She continued naming things as she noticed. She assigned Dale to vacuuming while she started cleaning the bathrooms. After six hours of intense work, Andi was climbing into her car. She was absolutely exhausted but had such a feeling of accomplishment. He had paid her extremely well, and she was glad because she had her eye on a special Christmas present for her grandparents. Lexus was waving from the living-room window. *What a precious little girl*, Andi thought as she headed home.

Dale walked through his house so overwhelmed that he couldn't stem the tears. The living room was clean and tidy. The kitchen was the cleanest it had been since he moved in. The floor wasn't gritty, and the countertops were gleaming. It smelled fresh, and Andi had made him a grocery list. *Wow, she's some woman*, he thought. Lexus was following him around, chatting a mile a minute. He walked into her bedroom, and it was clean and orderly. Now that everything was cleaned and in its place, her bedding stood out like a sore thumb. It was faded and too immature for her. He walked into his bedroom and was amazed at how peaceful it made him feel. The master bathroom was so clean that light seemed to bounce off the walls and floor. There were thick white towels and washcloths folded and hanging on the towel rack. He reached out to feel one. The tub and shower were gleaming, and the mirror was sparkling clean.

"I'm hungry, Daddy," said Lexus.

"Me too, baby. Let's go see what we can find."

They ate scrambled eggs and toast for dinner. After giving Lexus a bath, Dale sprayed detangler and combed out her hair. Lexie put on her new pajamas and climbed into her bed. She was asleep before Dale finished her story. He looked over at her little face and felt at peace for the first time in a very long time.

Dale had made arrangements for Andi to come back the following week. The basic cleaning was done, but he needed her help to replenish things the house really needed. As he walked around the house, he made mental notes to add to the shopping list.

The following day, he and Lex bought a real tree from the Boy Scouts at the corner. Lexie was so excited she couldn't sit still. The tree was a little big, but that just made it more exciting for both of them. He strung on the colored lights and realized it still looked a little anemic. He decided to wait for Andi to tell him what it needed.

"What do you want for Christmas, Kit Kat?"

Dale was expecting for her to roll out a list, but she turned to him very seriously and said, "I want a mommy."

Dale was so taken aback that he picked her up and held her on his lap. They turned all the lights off except the Christmas lights and sat quietly.

"I know you do, baby. But you know what? It's just you and me, Lexie."

She said, "I know, Daddy. But I still want a mommy. I'm the only one in kindergarten without a mom. There are lots of kids without a daddy, but everyone has a mommy."

He looked at her dark eyes and said, "I'm sorry, babe, but you're stuck with your dad."

Lexie hugged him, always so tenderhearted. She fell asleep in his arms while he pondered their future.

* * * * *

Living Water's Christmas program was scheduled for the next Sunday, and Becca had been chosen to sing a carol with sign language. Abby had taught her all the hand movements, and Becca practiced it till she had it perfect. Having just turned ten, she was growing very tall and slender. Her blonde hair was down the middle of her back.

Abby and Isaac had just discovered that Abby was expecting, and they had decided to tell Becca at the breakfast table. Becca jumped up and ran to hug Abby. "Oh, Mom, I'm so excited. What will we name the baby? Can we name her middle name a flower like you and Aunt Andi and Grammy and Mamaw?"

Isaac laughed and said, "What if it's a boy?"

Becca's face fell and said, "Oh, I don't know. There were never any boys, were there?" She sat pensively a minute, and a grin split her face as she snapped her finger and said, "I know! We could name him Phil."

"Phil?" said Abby and Isaac at the same time.

Becca said, "Yeah, short for Philodendron."

They all laughed hysterically as they went to dress for church.

* * * * *

Victoria had found her place to serve at Living Water. She felt the most comfortable with children, so she had volunteered to teach a class and help with special events. She was excited to attend the Christmas play and fellowship afterward. Making new friends didn't come naturally to her, but the people there were warm and had welcomed her with open arms.

Victoria called the children to line up. "Come on, kids. Does everyone have their white gloves on?" She looked at the twenty-five children nodding. Their little faces were flushed with excitement. They were dressed in their Sunday's best, all in black and white.

She had worked with them for weeks and weeks to learn "Joy to the World" on their handle bells. A CD of an orchestra and choir would play while they rang their bells. She held up cards with the words and chords. It wasn't rocket science, but it sounded great, and the children had practiced until they were confident.

They walked out on the stage and lined up, each one standing on the piece of masking tape Victoria had taped to the floor. They each held their bell to their chest and waited for her signal to begin.

Everyone clapped and cheered when they finished. The children took a bow and filed off in single file. Pastor Bob was standing at the end of the stage and gave her a thumbs-up as she walked by. "Great job, Victoria," he whispered with a smile. She smiled back and nodded as she herded her little flock back down the steps.

* * * * *

Abby knocked again on the dirty screen door. She tried to look through the window, but the glass was encrusted with dirt and grime. She turned the doorknob and eased the door open. "Mrs. Glascock? It's Abby from home health. Yoo-hoo, Mrs. Glascock, are you here?" She listened for any sound. She walked through the living room and peeked into the bedroom. The unmade bed was empty. She turned back and found a note on the dining-room table explaining Mrs. Glascock had to go to a funeral and wasn't able to reach Abby in advance to let her know.

Abby looked around at poor Mrs. Glascock's shabby home. It needed cleaning, and Abby knew she had no family. With a quick glance at the clock, Abby took off her coat and began straightening up.

She started in the kitchen, washing the few dishes in the sink, drying, and putting them away. She washed down the counters and table and swept the floor. She looked in the refrigerator and found it nearly empty. Nothing but ice trays in the freezer. She opened the cupboards to see if Mrs. Glascock had any food. Abby knew Mrs. Glascock lived on a very small check each month. She wrote herself a note to get some groceries from the food pantry at church. They tidied up the living room, made the bed, and tied up the trash, taking it with her as she left. She made a mental note to make some potato soup to bring back. Mrs. Glascock was such a dear soul. Abby delighted in helping her patients. Especially the ones who lived alone or were in reduced circumstances.

Her next stop was Maria Mendoza. She was a Hispanic patient that had just had a baby born with multiple medical issues. Abby pulled into the apartment complex and flipped open Maria's chart. It showed her to be addicted to opioids and a host of other things. As she got out of the car, she grabbed her mace. This neighborhood was definitely rough. Abby gingerly made her way up the darkened staircase, careful not to touch the hand railing. The whole area reeked of smoke, urine, and lingering unpleasant food odors. Abby knocked for the third time, calling out, "Maria, it's Abby the home health nurse."

The door was opened by a young boy with only a T-shirt and underpants on.

"Hello there, is Maria home?"

The boy shook his head no.

"Is there an adult here?"

He said, "No, only me."

"May I come in?"

The boy opened the door wider and let her in. Abby stood aghast at the condition of the home. "What's your name, sweetheart?"

"Jose."

"How old are you?"

"I'm four."

"Is your mom here?"

"No."

"Where is she?"

"I don't know."

"Why are you here alone?"

Jose shrugged. Abby stood dumbfounded, looking around. Roaches were crawling over the floor and countertops. The apartment smelled like rotting food. The trash can was full and flowed over the floor. She asked the boy, "How long have you been here alone?"

The little boy just stood looking at her. Abby walked through the apartment looking for clothes for him to put on. She fished a pen and paper out of her purse and wrote a note, taping it to the front door. Unable to find anything for Jose to wear, she took off her coat and wrapped him in it.

"How about you go get some lunch with me?"

He nodded excitedly. She quickly took him to the car and buckled him in the back seat with a seat belt. "Have you had anything to eat today?"

"No."

"Are you hungry?"

He nodded yes. After feeding him with french fries, chicken nuggets, and milk, she took him to the clinic to talk to Isaac. "What should I do with him?" she whispered.

Isaac called the police department, and they informed Abby to bring him in, and a foster family would be called in to take him until the mother could be found. Abby waited with Jose, and within an hour, a young couple in their midthirties came. Abby walked to her car, relieved as she had watched the couple interact with Jose. He willingly went right to them. Having experience as foster parents, they had brought a bag of clothes and a car seat. Abby was thankful as she drove home after an eventful day.

* * * * *

Andi was deeply touched at how Dale had tried to keep things tidy. After a quick cleaning, they had gone shopping with an ever-growing list. They had a fun time at Walmart and spent a small fortune replenishing some household items. They bought new glasses, a cookie sheet and hot mitts, a sugar bowl, a broom and dustpan, new sheets, bedspreads, towels, a snow shovel, and a bag of salt for the icy sidewalk. Dale was pleasant and humorous, and Andi enjoyed his company. Lexus hadn't asked for anything, which was a real surprise to Dale. She complimented him on how well he had trained her. Dale's face clouded with sadness and said, "If I'm honest, Andi, it's not because I've trained her well. It's because she's simply not used to being spoiled. I can count on one hand how many times I've taken her shopping."

Andi said, "Dale, I've made a lot of mistakes in my life, but God has been good to me and given me a chance to start over. You can too. You've been so blessed to have this beautiful daughter. It's obvious she loves you."

He nodded but didn't say much. On the way home, she invited him and Lexus to come to the Christmas program. He said he'd think about it.

Andi had helped Lexus pick out a new bedspread and curtains for her room. Lexus wanted Strawberry Shortcake, but Andi thought she would outgrow it too quickly, so she convinced her to get a different set in varying shades of pink and green. It looked great in her room. She'd even picked up a couple of pictures to hang on her walls. One was a ballerina in a beautiful tulle outfit, and one was a picture of a little girl in a bubble bath with her doll babies. Before Andi left, she helped them put tinsel and ornaments on the tree. Dale lifted Lexus high to set the angel on top. When Andi was ready to go, Lexus cried after her. Dale was deeply affected by this. He stood helpless and frustrated, not knowing what to do. He started to pick Lexi up, but Andi shook her head and took Lexi by the hand. She sat down in the rocker and pulled her into her lap. She rocked and talked softly to Lexus, who was hanging on for dear life. Dale had to fight tears watching Andi tenderly rocking his daughter. His heart turned over as he looked at Andi with different eyes. She was beautiful. He had thought of her as strong and independent, but now he saw her as feminine and very attractive. And she was a Christian. He wondered what her reaction would be when she found out he knew the Lord.

* * * * *

Abby was excited to have her entire family coming for Christmas dinner. Her mom, dad, Andi, and her grandparents were coming. Andi had invited Dale and Lexus. She had decorated for days and shopped for weeks.

Her new dining room trestle table and benches would seat sixteen. The Christmas tree was decorated with hundreds of white lights, ornaments, and wide red and gold ribbon woven through the branches. The house was permeated with the smell of turkey. They were preparing a feast, and Mamaw was bringing her famous four-layer homemade carrot cake. The family was looking forward to meeting Dale and Lexus. Andi and Dale had been seeing each other just as friends, and everyone knew this was not a date. But they were hoping for an opportunity to witness to him and make him feel welcome and a part of the family.

"Here comes Andi," said Becca.

Andi came in with her arms loaded down with packages. Isaac slipped out to carry the rest of her things in. Andi was looking forward to giving her gifts. She had worked over time and had made the extra money cleaning for Dale, so she was pleased to have been able to buy gifts she was proud of. She had gotten Becca a portable CD player and purple lava lamp for her room. She had gotten Mamaw and Papaw a propane fish fryer and a case of peanut oil. She could hardly wait to see their faces. She had gotten her mom and dad gift cards to Cracker Barrel, Olive Garden, and Outback Steakhouse. She knew she could never go wrong with gift cards. Her parents loved to eat out at this stage of their life. She had gotten Abby and Isaac tickets to the Redskins game. That had taken some fancy footwork, but she was thrilled to have pulled it off. She got Lexus a Bible storybook and a white bear like she and Abby had as kids. Now if everyone would come on, they could get the party started.

* * * * *

Abby was excited as they got ready to draw names for the home health patient. She and her coworkers had each submitted a name for the draw. Abby clapped her hands and shouted yay when Mrs. Glascock's name was drawn out of the jar. The whole staff would donate money to get Mrs. Glascock some much-needed Christmas gifts. Abby was so thankful that all of her coworkers were in unity over this tradition and very generous in their giving. Abby knew the bus picked up Mrs. Glascock every Tuesday for the senior center. While she was there, Abby would bring the gifts over and have them ready to surprise her when the bus brought her home.

Abby finished bagging up the wrappers and trash as she heard the bus pull up. She ran to open the door as Mrs. Glascock got her key out. "Surprise!" Abby called, and she jerked the door open.

"Well, hello, darling, isn't this a lovely surprise. What are you doing here today?"

"Merry Christmas, Mrs. Glascock. Every year we put the names of all our patients in a jar, and the one we draw out is the one who gets the Christmas gifts. And you won!"

Mrs. Glascock beamed, putting one hand to her chest. "Oh my word, I did? Why, I've never won a thing in my life. Not even bingo." She laughed. She stepped through the door and froze, completely shocked. Her drab living room had been changed into a cozy, delightful room. She had a new adjustable reading lamp and stand by her armchair. A soft cozy throw was over one arm. A lovely rug was on the floor, a soft gray blue with a border of small flowers. Her very old heavy gold drapes had been replaced with a pull-down shade with a scalloped bottom, and pull chord and soft sheers hung gracefully over top. The blinds were up, allowing sunlight to flood the previously dark room.

Abby pulled her by the hand into the kitchen. A new coffeepot sat on the countertop with a lovely glass canister set shining in a row. One jar was filled with sugar, one with flour, one with coffee, and one with teabags. The clear glass square jars fit flush against the back splash. New tea towels and hot mitts lay beside them, along with a stackable coffee-mug stand, each cup fitting snugly on top of the other.

"Oh, my dear, my dear, this is too much. I'm just overwhelmed." She reached out to hug Abby.

Abby kissed her cheek and said, "I'm so happy for you, Mrs. Glascock. And my grandma Esther made you some potato soup here on the stove and baked you a loaf of bread this morning."

"Well, that's fine, isn't it? My, my...well, I hope you won't make me eat alone."

Abby said, "I'm starving."

Mrs. Glascock's heart nearly burst with happiness, and she took off her coat and went to lay it across her bed. "Abby girl, there's more?"

"Ha-ha, yes, there is." Abby ran into the bedroom as Mrs. Glascock was looking at her new bedding. New sheets and pillowcases and a lovely new bedspread made her bedroom complete.

"I've never had such lovely things," she said as she felt the soft sheets. "I feel like a queen, I do." She laughed through her tears. "Come on, let's eat."

They walked arm in arm back through her tiny house to the kitchen.

* * * * *

Jerry felt lonely as he drove through town. He found himself fighting depression. The holidays were always a challenge for him. He had bought Becca a gift, but he longed to see her. He toyed with the idea all evening and finally dialed Isaac's number and asked him if he could deliver Becca's gift in person. Isaac and Abby were delighted and told him he was welcome. He decided to fly in two days after Christmas. Isaac and Becca went to pick him up at Washington Dulles. They were waiting at the luggage return when Becca spotted him. She took off running and cried, "Granddaddy!" as he swept her up in his arms.

"You're nearly as tall as me, Becca. Just look at you," he said as he held her by both arms. He could see his own daughter, Rebecca's, sweet face in Becca's. He thought of his precious wife, Louise. His heart ached as he thought of how she would adore this beautiful little girl. Becca was chatting a mile a minute as they linked arms and walked toward Isaac.

Isaac shook his hand warmly and said, "It's good to see you, Jerry. Merry Christmas."

Jerry's eyes watered as he said, "Thanks for letting me invite myself, Isaac. This means a lot to me."

Isaac said, "You're welcome to come anytime, Jerry. We have the room, and Becca dearly loves you."

Becca beamed at her granddad.

"How's Abby?" Jerry asked.

"She's doing great, and we have some news. Would you like to tell him, Bec?"

Becca nodded excitedly and said, "Oh, Granddaddy, you'll never guess. We're going to have a new baby. Mom's expecting, and it's due in August. Isn't that wonderful?" she said with her eyes sparkling.

Isaac and Jerry smiled at each other.

Becca added, "I hope it's a girl so we can name her a flower."

"Why a flower?" asked Jerry.

"Oh, Granddad, it's the coolest tradition. Mom's grandparents a gazillion years back all had girls. And they named all the girls with a flower name."

"Really?" said Jerry. "That's really different. What's Abby's name?"

Becca said, "Her name is Abigail Zinnia."

Jerry grinned and said, "What's Andi's name?"

Becca answered, "It's Andrea Marigold. So if it's a girl, I'm hoping Mom and Dad will continue the tradition."

He said, "Have you picked out a name yet?"

She said, "Not yet, but I know they haven't used Lilac or Tulip yet."

Jerry tried not to laugh as he watched her animated expressions. "What if it's a boy?" he asked

"Oh, that's easy," said Becca. "We're naming him Phil."

"Phil?" he asked, raising his eyebrows.

"Yes, for *philodendron.*"

Jerry's face registered shock, and they all three burst out laughing.

"Catch me up, Becca. Tell granddaddy what you've been up to."

"Well, I was assigned a project at school. We're learning about being an entrepreneur. Do you know what that is Granddaddy?"

"Yes, I do, peanut."

"Well, we had to pretend that we were starting a business and write all about it. I had to think for a long time to come up with an idea. Some of my friends wrote about opening their own beauty shop, and another wanted to start a pretzel shop business. I was starting to panic because I couldn't think of anything. Then Daddy advised me to just look inside my heart and not think about just writing a paper. But if I could really and truly do anything I wanted to, what would it be? So I decided I wanted to open a community soup kitchen. My teacher gave me an A. She was so excited about it that she encouraged me to go for it. So I did."

"What do you mean by go for it?"

"Well, I wrote a letter to every church in town and every business owner. Then I followed up with a meeting. I called and made an appointment to meet with all the preachers and storeowners. They were all real nice to me. And they all smiled and nodded a lot. I explained my goal, asking them if they would be willing to donate monthly for the supplies and if they would be willing to volunteer to serve once a month. The local newspaper agreed to do a write-up about it and to advertise which businesses were donating, as well as who was serving along with pictures. Then the local news heard about it, and we got on channel 3, and before long, other news channels jumped on it. So now we have donations coming in from all over the country, and I put the money in a special bank account. One of the local businessmen that owns the bakery had a building he lets us use rent-free. So we're feeding the homeless and poor people, widows, and families of people in jail."

Jerry's mouth hung open as Becca filled him in. He shook his head in amazement. "Becca boo, I'm so proud of you. What a smart cookie you are."

"Not really, Granddaddy. I certainly thank you, but the Lord gets all the credit."

Jerry reached back to pat her face and said, "I love you, baby girl. Don't you ever forget that."

"I won't. I love you too, and I'm so glad you're here."

"Jerry, are you hungry? Abby went to the after-Christmas sales with her mom, so why don't we grab some lunch out?"

"Let's go to the Lunch Box, Daddy. You'll love this place, Granddaddy. They have the best chocolate malts in town."

They were just finishing their lunch when Beebee walked by. "Well, hey there. How y'all doing?" asked Beebee with her friendly smile.

Isaac said, "Hello, Beebee, merry Christmas."

"Same to you, sweetie," said Beebee.

"I'd like to introduce you to my father. Dad, this is Betsy Brown. Beebee, this is Becca's grandfather, Jerry James."

Jerry stood and removed his cap. He smiled into Betsy's eyes and reached to shake her hand. "Very nice to meet you," said Jerry.

Isaac looked up in time to see Beebee blush. Isaac glanced over at Jerry to see definite interest in his eyes. *So that's the way wind blows?* thought Isaac. *Well, it's been five years since Louise passed away. I'm sure he's lonely.*

Beebee's husband had died of a heart attack thirteen years earlier. He had a drinking problem and had been abusive to Beebee in her early years. Beebee had always seemed so strong and independent, but seeing her blush warmed Isaac's heart.

"Jerry, Beebee is a real estate agent, the top salesperson in this area, I might add," said Isaac.

"Go on with you," said Beebee, and she waved him off.

"She sold me my house, Jerry," said Isaac.

Beebee beamed and said, "If you decide to move this way, I hope you'll look me up, Jerry."

Jerry said, "Do I have to wait to move here to look you up?"

Beebee turned red and fumbled with her purse.

"I'll be here a few days, Beebee. I'd sure be delighted to take you to dinner one evening."

Beebee looked at Isaac to rescue her, and Isaac laughed and stepped back, holding up both hands. "You guys are on your own. I'll meet you in the car, Jerry. Bye, Beebee. Come on, Bec, we'll wait for granddaddy in the car."

Jerry strutted out to the car and climbed in. Isaac started the SUV and said, "Well, now, did you get a dinner date?"

"Yep. We're having dinner tomorrow evening, but you'll have to give me directions to her place. She offered to pick me up since I was visiting, but I told her a gentleman always escorts the lady."

Isaac laughed and said, "Where are you going?"

"She said she wanted to go to the Diamond Back."

"Nice place. They have great steaks," said Isaac.

"Granddaddy, can I go too?" asked Becca.

"Not this time, sweetheart, I have a date."

* * * * *

Word had spread quickly that Isaac and Abby were having a sleigh-riding party with a big bonfire. The hill behind their house was perfect for sledding. Isaac had taken a few trees down earlier in the season for the sole purpose of making it a great sledding spot. He and a few friends from church had gathered wood for the burn barrel. It would make a wonderful place to warm up. There were old-fashioned Flexible Flyer sleds, toboggans, plastic sleds, inner tubes, and everything in between. The length of the hill was enough to cause a thrill, but not long enough to be too long to walk back up.

Abby and Andi had made a vat of hot chocolate to help warm everyone up. They also were rotating gloves, running the wet ones back to the house to be thrown into the clothes dryer. The neighbors in the Gap had been invited too, and they even talked Dot Kingsley into a ride down. Her laughter echoed down the Gap. The kids were having the time of their life. They would all sleep good that night.

* * * * *

Beebee looked at herself in the mirror for the tenth time. "You're an old fool, Betsy Brown. Just look at you, all excited over a date." She had splurged on a new outfit. She had on a pale-pink cashmere turtleneck with a gorgeous pink-and-navy silk scarf tied around her neck. The lady at the counter showed her how to tie it elegantly. She had on navy slacks and slip-on loafers. She chose simple gold hoop earrings, her favorite gold tennis bracelet, and gold charm bracelet. She had painted her nails a buff pink. She looked at herself critically in the mirror and finally laughed at herself and said, "This is as good as it gets, old girl."

She sat musing in front of her dressing table when she heard a car pull into the driveway. Beebee opened the door, and Jerry stood holding a dozen roses. "Hi," he said softly.

Beebee smiled and said, "Hi."

They stood for a moment when Jerry said, "It's chilly out here. Can I come in?"

Beebee blushed and giggled. She could have kicked herself for acting like a schoolgirl. "Of course, come in, come in," she said as she stepped back into the foyer.

"I hope this won't seem too forward of me, but you look lovely, really lovely. I brought you some roses, but they certainly don't do you justice," he said, smiling.

She stared at the roses and turned to hide her face. She sniffled and said, "I'm sorry, Jerry. It's just that I've never had a dozen roses before."

"Not ever?" asked Jerry. He thought of how many times he'd gotten Louise flowers in their lifetime.

"Not ever," she said, smiling a watery smile.

"I hope you'll excuse me," said Jerry, "but your husband must have been a fool."

Beebee laughed and said, "You have no idea. Come in while I put these lovely things in water."

Jerry followed her into the kitchen as she got a vase out from under the cabinet. "Beebee, is your real name Betsy?" he asked.

"No, it's Elizabeth, but my family called me Betsy. Then when I married, my last name was Brown, so I got nicknamed Beebee," she explained.

"Do you mind if I call you Elizabeth?" asked Jerry.

Beebee stopped arranging the flowers and turned to look at him. "Why would you want to do that?"

Jerry smiled into her eyes and said, "Because I think *Elizabeth* is a beautiful, feminine name, and it suits you better."

Beebee felt herself flush and said, "Jerry, what am I going to do with you?"

The waiter had cleared their table as they sat with coffee chatting about their prior lives. Suddenly Jerry looked around and realized the restaurant was nearly empty. He looked at his watch and said, "I think they're going to start blinking the lights if we don't get out of here."

Jerry pulled into Beebee's driveway and said, "I can't remember when I've had such an enjoyable weekend. Would you consider seeing me again, Elizabeth?"

Beebee didn't hesitate and said, "Yes, Jerry, anytime you're this way, you give me a call."

He looked crestfallen and said, "I don't know when I'll be back."

"Do you have e-mail?" she asked.

Jerry laughed and said, "I have never even touched a computer. I guess I'm a dinosaur."

Beebee said, "Oh, Jerry, you should get one. They're easy to learn, and you would enjoy surfing the web, and we could e-mail."

Jerry thought about his lonely life. He had been bored and out of sorts for months. But a computer? His mind was spinning with possibilities. He wanted to kiss Elizabeth's sweet lips and shocked himself with the thought.

"What does that look mean?" asked Beebee.

"It means I'm going to buy a computer, that's what," said Jerry. "But I don't know how I'll learn it."

"When do you go home, Jerry?"

"My plane leaves day after tomorrow."

"Well, if you're not busy tomorrow evening, why don't you come over, and I'll show you around the net a little?"

"You'll show me around what?" asked Jerry.

Beebee laughed and said, "I'll show you some basic computer skills."

"Sounds great. What time?"

"Are you sure I won't be interfering with your time with Becca?"

"Yes, Elizabeth, I'm sure. Becca's out of school right now for Christmas break, and we've had some wonderful time together. Plus, I'm spending the whole day with her tomorrow."

"All right then, come over about five thirty, and I'll throw in supper."

* * * * *

Isaac and Becca helped Abby load the boxed groceries in the back of her SUV. "Be sure to load them in according to drop off. We're going to Mrs. Glasscock's first so put that box in last." Abby was checking her list of home health patients that her church was helping.

Isaac said, "Mrs. Thompson called and said to stop by the bakery on the way. She has bread and goodies for your patients."

* * * * *

Andi and Abby were painting the nursery when Andi said, "Abby, I know God's Word is true, and I know God has forgiven me for all my sins, but two abortions are just too much. I've broken all the commandments. I know He loves me, but He has to because He's God. He has to love everyone, but the guilt of my past haunts me and makes me feel unworthy. I know my babies are in heaven, but it really hurts to even think about it. I dream about the baby I gave away all the time."

Abby stopped painting and turned to her sister. "Andi, I want to tell you something really important. There is absolutely nothing we can do to make God love us more. But there's also nothing we can do that will make God love us less. Every sin you have ever committed—past, present, and even in the future—has already been taken care of on the cross. The work Jesus did on the cross makes us righteous. Remember when you used to say I was the good daughter and you were the bad? There's nothing good in me, Andi. It's all Him. God is not a man that He should lie. His Word is true regardless of what we think or feel. Our emotions try to rule us all the time. Psalms 103 says, 'He forgives all of our iniquities as far as the east is from the west.' I never really realized the impact of east to west until someone shared with me that the earth has a north and south pole.

They're actually latitude and longitude points on the globe. But east to west goes around forever.

"God forgives us of all we ever did, all we're doing now, and all the sins we'll ever do in the future. The blood of Jesus makes us whiter than snow. When we miss the mark, we need to repent, but it's so we can keep an open heaven and maintain sweet fellowship. If your child sins, it doesn't mean he's no longer your child. It's the same with God. His Word is true. You need to establish that even though you don't understand it all. You've chosen to believe that the Bible is the truth no matter what. The Bible has to be our plumb line and our rule book. Otherwise, everything in life becomes relative. That's why there are so many mixed-up, depressed people today who are desperately looking for truth. There's right and wrong, and all the answers we'll ever need are in that book. You just have to forgive yourself. All of us fall short of the mark, Andi. But the blood of Jesus covers us and makes us righteous in God's eyes."

Andi nodded and continued painting. She needed time to digest what her sister had just told her. A few minutes later, she said "Abby, can I share something with you in secret? I want to try to find my child. Just so I can have peace that he or she is cared for and okay."

Abby said, "Oh I don't know about that, Andi. What if you found out…well, that things aren't what you hoped for? Can you handle that? And what if you can't find the baby? Can you handle that too? I just don't want you to get hurt."

Andi stopped painting and stared out the window.

Abby's heart went out to her sister. She said, "Andi, your life has completely turned around. You're a wonderful teacher, your finances are stable, you're healthy, and you're involved at church. Let's spend some time praying and asking God to direct you about this. If He's in it, you'll find your baby. And if He's not, then He'll give you peace."

Andi turned to hug Abby.

* * * * *

"How's Dale doing?" asked Abby.

Andi replied, "He's still drinking some, but overall, he's doing remarkably well."

"Does the drinking discourage you?"

"Not at all. I know he's hurting. I was a drunk, remember? I know what the holidays can do, but I see a softening in him, Abby. When he opens up, I'm really astounded at his depth and knowledge."

"Have you had a chance to witness to him?"

"Not in a strong way, but I do talk about the Lord and my faith, and he knows I used to drink and all that."

Abby asked gently, "Do you have feelings for him?"

Andi replied without hesitation, "I think he's wonderful."

"Do you know if he feels the same about you?"

"Frankly I think he's fighting it."

"Fighting you or fighting God?"

After thinking on it a moment, Andi replied, "He thinks it's both, but it's God in me that he's fighting. But yes, I do have feelings for him, strong ones, and I absolutely adore Lexus."

"It worries me a little that you two have bonded this quickly and this deeply. I mean, it will break both of your hearts if things go south."

"I'm just going to take each day and trust the Lord."

Abby smiled at her sister and said, "I love you, Andi."

"I know," said Andi as she smiled warmly into her sister's eyes. "And it's what's kept me all these years. But if Dale doesn't show some interest soon, then I'm not spending any more time waiting and spinning my wheels. I'm lonely, Abby, and I want marriage and children. I believe the Lord has that plan for me. I don't want to continue to press my attention on someone who is clearly not interested in that type of relationship."

After painting quietly for a while, Andi spoke again, "Mike Ramey asked me out for a date."

Abby spun around excitedly. "Really? What's your hesitation? He's handsome as all get out. He's your age, single, a strong Christian, he has a good job. Hello? Am I missing something?"

Andi laughed and said, "I know, I know. It's just that I really like Dale. But I said yes."

Abby was excited as she peppered her sister with questions about where they were going and what she would wear. The time sped by, and they were finished painting before they were finished talking.

* * * * *

Jerry followed his nose to the kitchen. Abby was frying bacon.

"Good morning, Jerry. This will be your last morning with us, so I wanted to fix you a good breakfast. How does bacon and eggs, pancakes. and grits sound?"

Jerry answered her by kissing her cheek. He leaned against the kitchen counter sipping his coffee. As much as he loved his sweet Rebecca and as painful as it was to have lost her and Louise both, it comforted his heart greatly that Isaac had found love twice in his life. Abby was open and sweet and obviously loved Becca. *Maybe I can find love again too*, he mused.

* * * * *

"Okay, this is called the mouse," said Beebee.

Jerry was being instructed, and he was intent to learn.

"Now what you see on the screen is called the cursor, and you move it like this," she said.

Jerry said, "It's difficult to concentrate when my tummy is overly full."

Beebee laughed and said, "You did eat like a horse." She had fixed pinto beans with ham and a pan of corn bread.

Jerry patted his tummy and said, "If I backfire, just stick me out on the porch."

Beebee laughed hard and said, "Lord, Jerry, what I am going to do with you?"

* * * * *

Isaac and Abby hugged Jerry goodbye and said, "It's been such a great visit, Jerry. Please come again anytime. You're so, so welcome."

"Well, now it might be sooner than you think," he said, smiling.

They sat up late last night talking about Elizabeth and the computer training and the possibilities of a relation growing. Becca hugged him and walked him to the car. "Granddaddy, thank you so much for my opal ring and necklace. Mom and Dad never give me real jewelry, but I'm glad you think I'm grown up."

He hugged her long and kissed her forehead. "Goodbye, sweet girl, I'll be in touch."

They waved as he pulled out of their driveway.

* * * * *

Jerry had been home three weeks when he received a sale flyer that electronics were on sale. He sat staring at the computers. "That's it!" he said, slapping his kitchen table. "Today's the day."

Jerry's mind was whirling as he drove into his driveway. The salesclerk looked like a kid, but he was a plethora of information. He had written down his name and number on a card to give to him. "Call me if you run into any problems, Mr. James, and I'll talk you right through it."

Jerry could hardly wait to e-mail Elizabeth.

Jerry sat cross-legged on the floor, attempting to hook up his new toy. "It's dummy-proof," Todd had told him. "Just match color to color."

Jerry rolled his eyes and crawled up his chair to stand. His stiff joints were screaming at him. He picked up the phone and dialed the number. "Todd, this is Jerry. I hooked up the colors, and it still doesn't work."

"Did you turn it on?"

"Uh, sheesh, I forgot to do that," said Jerry, feeling like a stupid old dinosaur.

"That's okay, Mr. James, happens all the time. See ya."

Jerry felt embarrassed and pushed the on button. Suddenly the computer lit up and asked him questions. *Oh man, I'm clueless,* he thought. He dialed the phone again, "Todd? I turned it on, and now it's asking me questions."

Todd laughed and said, "How about I stop by after work and fix you up?"

"You'd do that for me?"

"Sure, if my dad got a computer, I'd want somebody to help him. Where do you live?"

Jerry gave him directions, and Todd said, "No prob, see ya later."

* * * * *

Beebee was busy on her computer when someone knocked on her door. The florist delivery man came in with flowers. "Delivery for Elizabeth Brown," he said. A smile split her face as her coworkers piled in her room.

"Elizabeth?? Since when are you called Elizabeth? You're holding out on us, Beebee. Who are these from?" asked Marcie loudly.

Beebee opened the card when obnoxious Marcie grabbed it out of her hand. Marcie read in a loud voice, "Dear Elizabeth, roses are red, violets are blue, I've never known anyone as precious as you. Love, Jerry."

Beebee was livid with Marcie but chose not to react as she smiled at the rest of her coworkers.

"Well, aren't we closemouthed?" said Marcie. "Who's Jerry? And why does he call you Elizabeth?"

Beebee smiled and said, "He's a friend."

Everyone laughed as Beebee turned her back on them and continued working at her computer.

"I think we've been dismissed, girls," said Marcie.

Beebee said, "Would you mind closing the door as you leave?" She tucked the florist card safely in her wallet as she sat staring at the beautiful violets. *Jerry, what am I going to do with you?* she thought.

* * * * *

Andi sat at her desk preparing report cards as her students were reading. They had been antsy all day, but the spring weather was so gorgeous it was distracting her as well.

"Ms. Alexander?"

Andi looked up to see Tracey raising her hand.

"Yes, Tracey?"

Tracey shyly said, "You haven't announced who your special helper would be today."

Andi smiled and said, "Would you like to be my helper today, Tracey?"

Tracey turned bright red as she nodded excitedly.

"All right, you may go dust the erasers."

Tracey shot out of her seat and scooted up to the blackboard to grab the erasers.

Andi had a God-given gift to teach, and her students loved her. She had no problem maintaining order, but her love for the children was obvious. They craved strict parameters, which she had no problem issuing. Every day a different student was selected to be her special helper. It was a coveted position for the students and an honor to be chosen.

Andi glanced at her students' faces and again thought of the child she had given up for adoption. *My child would be six years old, Lord. Did I have a son or a daughter? Is he well cared for and loved?* She had come to absolute dead-ends in her search. Because she had chosen to know nothing about her child at birth, all the documents she had signed were ironclad. Andi knew she would never have the chance to find her child, but there was one thing she could do for her child, and that was cover him with prayer until the day she died. She prayed for her baby every single day and would continue. It gave her great peace.

* * * * *

"I'd like to take a week off Sam," said Beebee.

Sam smiled warmly at Beebee and said, "You'll get no lip from me, Beebee. You deserve a vacation. Can I be nosy and ask where you're going?"

Beebee smiled and said, "I'll keep it to myself."

Sam laughed and said, "Jerry's been out here half a dozen times, Beebee. I take it you've fallen for him."

Again Beebee just smiled.

"I'm glad for you, Bee. You deserve it."

Beebee smiled warmly and said, "Thanks, Sam."

Beebee got off the plane and walked through the airport to baggage claim. She could see Jerry pacing and looking at his watch. She walked up behind him and tapped him on the shoulder. He whirled around and threw his arms around her, hugging her tightly then swinging her around before setting her on her feet.

"Jerry"—she laughed hard—"what am I going to do with you?"

Jerry leaned his forehead against hers and said, "I'm sure we'll think of something."

Beebee pushed him away and said, "You behave yourself, Jerry James."

Jerry quickly kissed her on the lips and said, "Yes, ma'am." He retrieved her luggage and said, "Right this way, my dear. I'm so glad you came, Elizabeth. I've wanted to share my life here with you."

He pulled into the Holiday Inn and said, "Are you sure you won't stay at my house? I have two guestrooms. We're adults, Elizabeth. You know I would never ever take advantage of you."

"Now, Jerry, we've been over this. I think it's best that we don't give the enemy even a chance for gossip. We want to be a good witness to your neighbors and friends. Now it's all settled. Tell me your plans."

"My plans are holding you in my arms, showing you my favorite places here in town, holding you in my arms, dinner out, church, holding you in my arms."

Beebee was thrilled and assured him the plans sounded wonderful. He got her checked in and kissed her good-night. "Are you sure you don't want something to eat?" he asked.

"No, Jerry. I just need a hot shower and some rest."

"Okay, you've got my number if you need me. I'll pick you up at 8:00 a.m., and we'll go to breakfast."

* * * * *

Isaac's cell phone rang while he was examining old Mr. Jenkins at the clinic. Mr. Jenkins was Isaac's favorite patient. He was ninety-seven years old and sound as a dollar. He had no dementia, could read without glasses, and could hear a pin drop. He still worked a garden and kept him and Abby supplied with fresh vegetables.

Normally, Isaac would ignore his cell, but Abby was due any day. He looked at caller ID; it was Abby's mother, Helen. "Hello," said Isaac.

"Isaac, Abby's water broke. Her contractions are irregular, about twenty minutes apart."

Isaac hung up, excited, and said, "Mr. Jenkins, my wife's in labor."

Mr. Jenkins shook his hand and said, "I'll pray for her, son."

Isaac had shared with Mr. Jenkins before about what had happened to Rebecca, and he knew he was a little anxious about Abby's pregnancy.

"Keep your eyes on Jesus, son. Not the baby Jesus born humble and lowly in a manger and not the crucified Lamb. But you keep your eyes on the Jesus that John saw on the isle of Patmos whose eyes are like a flame of fire and hair as white as wool with feet like brass. You go on now. I'll be fine."

Isaac felt his faith rising. He grabbed Mr. Jenkins's hand and shook it hard. "Thank you, Mr. Jenkins, thank you so much." He jerked off his stethoscope and took off running down the hall.

He prayed for Abby all the way home. He refused to let fear overtake him. Instead, he began to pray, *Please, God, protect Abby and the baby*. He was nervous when he ran into the house. Seeing Abby sitting so calmly in the rocker calmed him immediately.

Seeing him, Abby said, "Oh, honey, I'm all right, come here."

He knelt down and wrapped his arms around her waist, laying his head on her lap. She stroked his hair and said, "Father, I speak the peace of Jesus over Isaac right now in Jesus's name. I come against this spirit of fear that has tried to raise its lying head. We thank You for our baby, Lord. Thank You for a normal, uneventful labor and delivery for Your glory. Amen."

Isaac reached up to kiss her. "How close are the contractions? Let's time them."

She said, "I don't want to go to the hospital till I have to."

"I know, honey, but since your water broke, we really don't have a choice. We need to get you into a sterile environment. Let's go."

Helene was waiting in the background. She had packed Abby's bag, tidied the house, made arrangements for Becca, called Andi and the rest of the family, and was excited for her first grandbaby to arrive. Abby and Isaac had decided to ask Helene, Mamaw Esther, and Andi to attend the birth. It would mean so much to them.

Andi called Dale to let him know Abby was about to give birth. They had become close friends and had really enjoyed getting to know each other. Andi was thrilled as she shared with Dale and couldn't contain her emotions. As they were hanging up, Dale shocked her into silence by saying, "Please tell Isaac that I'll be praying for Abby." He hung up before she could say anything. She thanked God for this breakthrough. The weekend before she had been cleaning for him, she found an open Bible on his bedside table. She wanted to ask him about it but felt a check in her spirit not to—not yet. She and her family and Bible study group had been praying faithfully for him, and she could see changes. She prayed all the way to the hospital.

Abby lay in bed panting as the doctor examined her. He told her, "You're nine centimeters, Abby. You can't push yet, or you'll tear."

Abby's face contorted as she leaned forward to push when Isaac got in her face.

"No!" he shouted. "Don't push, breathe with me—pant, pant, pant."

She was sweating, and her pupils were dilated. Andi was clearly shaken with her sister's pain. Mamaw Esther was softly praying, and Helene was flitting around with ice chips and a cool washcloth.

"Hang in there, Abby, you're doing great, just a little while longer," said Isaac.

An hour later, Abby—flushed-faced with her hair plastered to head—screamed with the last push as a big baby boy slid into the doctor's hands. Isaac cut the cord and placed the baby in Abby's arms. Everyone in the room was crying. Abby started speaking softly to the baby when he stopped crying and turned his head toward her. "Hey there, big boy. Hey, baby. You're okay. Hi, sweetheart. Do you know mommy's voice?"

Isaac was unashamedly crying.

The doctor said, "I need him for just a few minutes, then you all can hold him."

The baby weighed in at ten pounds, two ounces, and twenty-two inches long. He had a head full of thick black hair. Mamaw Esther went out to get Papaw Thomas. Everyone was crying and talking all at once.

Andi said, "What's his name, sis?"

Everyone turned expectantly to Abby and Isaac.

"We've chosen the name *Aaron*," said Isaac.

"And his middle name?" asked Andi, grinning.

Abby looked at Papaw and said, "It's Aaron Thomas."

Papaw choked up and said in a hoarse voice, "What an honor." He reached for the baby and held him up as an offering to the Lord and pronounced blessings over him, and Mamaw Esther anointed him with oil. Everyone bowed their head as Isaac and Abby prayed over him, dedicating his life to the Lord.

Andi's mind went to the day she was in the delivery room. How different that day was. She prayed, "Lord, You have a plan for our lives. If only we would listen and obey You. You long to bless us abundantly, but sin separates us. You're a just and merciful God. Thank You for this precious life. And thank You for watching over my baby."

* * * * *

"When are you going to introduce me to your family Andi?" asked Mike. "You've met my whole family."

Andi silently sighed. *What in the world is wrong with me?* Andi wondered. *This man is a prince. He's a good man, and he really likes me.* But Andi constantly compared him to Dale. She had fun with Mike. He was active and loved to go and do. He was always coming up with fun adventures. Not too many men she knew were such great planners. He sent her flowers. They'd gone to a basketball game, football, the movies, out to dinner, he loved to try new foods. Andi had never eaten Thai food before. The weekend before, they had gone up in a hot-air balloon. He seemed to have endless energy. Now he wanted her to hike part of the Appalachian Trail. Andi drew the line at that one. She was definitely not interested in walking her legs off. Hadn't he ever heard of bugs and snakes? She knew she was holding back and knew it was unfair to Mike.

"We'll go see my parents this weekend," she replied.

He smiled and hugged her. Andi had only allowed him to kiss her a few times. Mike was a little frustrated, and she didn't blame him. *Lord, direct me. I'm not getting any younger, and I don't want to blow this.*

Andi still cleaned Dale's house on a regular basis and he was always there as he worked from home. They had long easy chats, and they did things together with Lexus. Andi loved her time with Dale and Lexus. Although he was completely kind and attentive, he had never seemed interested in anything other than friendship.

* * * * *

Jerry and Beebee were having dinner at Jerry's favorite restaurant. "I can't believe this week is over already," said Jerry wistfully.

"I've enjoyed every minute of it, Jerry. I can't even begin to tell you how badly I've needed this."

They smiled warmly into each other's eyes as Jerry reached across the table for her hand.

"Do you ever think of getting out of real estate, Elizabeth? I know you're really good at sales, but do you ever long for a gentler pace?"

Beebee looked off into space and said, "Well, if truth were to be told, I've always had a dream of opening a B&B."

Jerry stared into her blue eyes and said, "What's to stop you?"

"Oh, Jerry, I can't change horses at this stage of my life."

"Sure, you could."

"No, I couldn't. Be reasonable."

"Why? Why should we be reasonable, Elizabeth? Haven't we been reasonable our whole lives? Let me share this dream with you. Let's follow our dream. Let's follow our heart."

Beebee smiled at Jerry and said, "What am I going to do with you?"

"I'll tell you what you're going to do. You're going to change your name to Elizabeth James. Marry me, Elizabeth. I'm in love with you. I'll sell my house and move to Virginia. Nothing's holding me there. Sell your house, and we'll pool our resources and open a B&B. Think of it, Elizabeth. We'll live there, and I'll plant beautiful flower beds with an iron arch covered with wisteria where couples can get married. We'll have beautiful suites that you can decorate with your elegant, homey touch. We'll provide breakfast. I'm the best omelet maker this side of the Mississippi. With your networking, we'll have a waiting list."

Elizabeth's eyes shone with excitement. She squeezed his hand and said, "Oh, Jerry, my mind is spinning with possibilities. But such change… I don't know."

"Marry me, Elizabeth. Let me take care of you. Let's grow old together."

Elizabeth didn't try to hide her tears as she nodded yes. Jerry pulled a box out of his jacket. Elizabeth's eyes flew to his. He opened the box to reveal a lovely sapphire surrounded with diamonds. "This stone reminded me of your exquisite blue eyes." He slipped out of the booth and came to her side on bended knee. He slipped the ring on her finger. "Grow old with me. The best is yet to be."

* * * * *

Saturday morning, Andi was cleaning Dale's house. Lexus had spent the night with a little friend from school, and Dale was working in his home office. Andi rolled the vacuum cleaner into Dale's room. She stripped his bed and was putting on fresh linens when she spied a guitar propped up in the corner of the bedroom. Dale had never mentioned playing, but then again, they never really talked about things too personal. Dale's Bible lay open again on his bedside table. She picked up his Bible and flipped through. She was shocked to see passages underlined and highlighted. Andi saw movement out of the corner of her eye and jumped when she saw Dale leaning against the doorjamb.

"I'm so sorry, Dale," she stuttered with embarrassment. "I was totally out of order to pick up your Bible. This is your personal space. I've never done anything like this before. I hope you believe me and can forgive me." The words rushed out of Andi's mouth.

Dale said, "Whoa, slow down, Andi. I'm not upset with you at all. As a matter of fact, you're the one that has a right to be upset with me."

"What do you mean?" asked Andi.

Dale said, "Let's go into the living room and talk."

Andi followed Dale mutely into the living room. Dale sat across from her and said, "Andi, you've been witnessing to me for a year now. I don't know how to tell you this, and I hope you will forgive me, but I received Jesus as my Savior when I was thirteen years old. I've never shared anything with you about my past, and it's time, if you're interested in listening."

Andi nodded but remained quiet.

"I was raised in a Christian home. I have two brothers, Neil and Patrick, and one sister, Claire. My parents were both Christians, as well as my grandparents. I'm sure you realize with a name like O'Reilly that we're Irish. My grandparents were born in Ireland in a little area called Glebe Hill. My mother moved to the States and met my father, who shared Jesus with her. They married and raised us to believe in Jesus.

"I went to a church camp one summer with a friend, and it was there I asked Jesus to be my Savior. It was a radical change in my life, and I felt called to the ministry even as a very young man. Not your typical preacher in a pulpit type, more like jail ministry or reaching alcoholics. I certainly didn't know then that I'd become one myself. I met my wife in that youth group. Her name was Laurie, and she was a vivacious teen and on fire for God. We fell in love and married right out of high school. We both struggled through college but managed to graduate. It was tough working and going to school, but we were both determined to finish. I landed a good job as an IT man with a really successful computer company, and it put my ministry dreams on the back burner. We were typical yuppies. We had a nice home and were involved in our church. Laurie taught a Sunday school class there, and I was a deacon. Laurie wanted to start a family. After being married two years, we began to try, but Laurie couldn't conceive. After a long saga of heartache, we ended up adopting Lexus."

Andi's heart started beating painfully against her ribs. She interrupted Dale with, "Where did you get your baby? What state? When's her birthday?"

Dale was taken aback at Andi's abrupt tone. He answered, "Our attorney handled everything. Our pastor made the connection. We lived in Ohio at the time, and we weren't allowed to know her birthplace. Her birth date is August 17. Why are you asking me these questions, Andi?"

Andi felt ridiculous as she realized this couldn't be her child.

Dale walked over to her. "Andi, tell me what's going on."

She replied in a shaky voice, "Can you tell me your story first? I'm sorry, Dale. I shouldn't have interrupted you. We both obviously have some baggage. I really appreciate you trusting me to share, Dale. I'll tell you my story later." Dale stared at her when she said, "Please Dale, bear with me."

Dale sat back down on the couch watching Andi. They sat in silence a couple of minutes, recovering from Andi's outburst. Dale continued, "We adopted Lexus as a newborn. She was five days old when our pastor brought her to our home. She had just turned five years old when my wife and I were on a motorcycle trip with our biker's club from church when we got hit broadside by a speeding driver. Laurie was killed instantly, and I was injured badly with multiple broken bones. I was heartbroken, angry, and confused for a long time, and I allowed bitterness to consume me. I started drinking to dull the pain, and the rest is history. God brought you into my life, and your lifestyle was a balm to my soul, Andi. Your walk with God and your openness about your uncomplicated relationship with God made me homesick. I started reading the Word, and my heart began to heal. I've prayed and repented, and you're largely responsible for my turnaround."

Andi couldn't stop herself from crying. Dale reached over and took her hand and pulled her up. He embraced her in a sweet hug as she continued crying on his shoulder.

"I'm a mess." Andi laughed.

Dale said, "Hey, I've cried a few tears myself in the last few weeks, and I'm not too proud to admit it."

Andi smiled a watery smile and said, "I have things to tell you too, Dale. I hope you won't judge me too harshly."

"Are you kidding me? I would never judge you. Besides, your past is between you and God, Andi. You don't owe me anything."

"I want to tell you a little about my past, Dale. I don't need to go into all the details. My sins are under the blood, but there are some things I want you to know." She took a deep breath and said, "I was raised in a Christian home too. My sister Abby got saved as a young teen at church camp, but I was the black sheep of the family with a rebellious streak a mile wide. I purposed in my heart to have nothing to do with religion. I ran from God as fast as I could. I did every sin imaginable, and some I'm deeply regretful over. But like you, the mercy of God extended even to me. My family was ruthless at praying for me, and I finally yielded my heart to God. I repented. He forgave me, and I now try to live my life solely for Him. In my jaded mind, I thought being a Christian meant a long list of rigid rules that I knew I couldn't keep. So many Christians I knew tried to make me feel guilty over swimming in a pool, wearing shorts, watching a movie, playing football, and other equally ridiculous things. It was a club, and if you didn't fit their profile, you were shunned. Of course, I know better now. I've learned what my authority is as a believer and realize in their ignorance they were just walking in the only light they knew. But it certainly didn't compel me to want to join their club.

"When I was twenty-two years old, I became pregnant and decided to give up my baby for adoption. My life was such a wreck. I didn't know the Lord then and miraculously did not have an abortion, which is a whole different story in itself. My baby was born

August 12 six years ago. I chose at the time of birth to know nothing about my child. I thought it would be less painful that way. I don't know if I had a son or daughter or who adopted my child. I hired an attorney to try to find my baby, but I signed some ironclad paperwork and finally had to give my baby to the Lord once and for all. I still pray daily and am hoping for a miracle someday to meet and explain and ask forgiveness. I was young and stupid and knew I'd make a terrible mother. That's why I asked about Lexus. But their birthdays aren't the same."

Dale stared at Andi with his mouth open. The hair stood up on the back of his neck. "Andi, I have to ask you something." His eyes bore into hers. He leaned forward and said nearly in a whisper, "Please tell me your middle name."

Andi jumped up, putting her hand to her throat. "Why are you asking me this, Dale?"

"Please just tell me."

"It's Marigold," she said.

"Wait here."

Dale ran from the room as Andi stood trembling. Before she could form a prayer, he ran back in and shoved a paper into her hands. Andi looked down at Lexus's birth certificate. Her name was Lexus Lilly O'Reilly, and her birth date was August 12. She looked up at him in shock.

He said, "Her real birthday is August 12, but since we got her on the seventeenth, Laurie always celebrated her birthday on the date we got her. Our pastor said that the birth mother requested we give the baby a middle name of a flower as a part of her birth family's heritage. I thought it was ridiculous, but Laurie insisted we do this as part of her heritage and to honor the birth mother for giving her up for adoption."

Andi stared at the birth certificate. "Dale... Lexus...she's my baby. No wonder she looks so much like my mother. I can't believe it. I just can't believe it." She was shaking so violently Dale sat her back down on the chair. He knelt down beside her.

"Are you okay?"

Her face had gone white as a sheet. He went to get her a bottle of water. Andi was in shock.

"Come here, Andi, lie down on the couch." He covered her with a blanket.

"Don't leave me, Dale," she said, squeezing his hand.

"I won't," he said. He pulled the chair up next to her. No words were necessary between them. They both were in shock. Andi finally drifted to sleep as Dale sat staring at her lovely face.

He prayed, *God, You knew it all along. Your grace is amazing.* His mind went to his sweet Laurie. Her heart was so pure that he knew she would be okay with Andi, the birth mother of his little Lexus. His mind raced as he looked down at Andi's features. He could see so much of Lexus. Even the way they walked was alike. *How could I have been so blind?* he wondered. *Lord, now what? Andi and I have been through so much together. I love her, Lord, but I don't know how she feels about me. I don't want to rush her. Help me to court her and make her fall head over heels in love me.*

Dale and Lexus had been attending church regularly. Dale had even started writing worship songs again. He had been through so much that his misery had become his ministry, and the lyrics of his songs bore out the depth of his love and gratitude to God.

* * * * *

Renee loved the feel of the wind in her hair. She felt free galloping across the field on her sweet mare, Robin. Jonathan bought it for her as a wedding gift. The day he moved into his new house at the farm, he and Renee had Pastor Bob to perform their wedding in the living room with Isaac and Abby as witnesses. Jonathan said he wanted them to spend the first night together in their own home. They weren't interested in a honeymoon. They just wanted to get on with their lives. It had taken some adjusting for both of them. Jonathan had been a bachelor for many years, and Renee wasn't used to being treated well. Jonathan had to gently remind her over and over that he didn't expect the house to be spotless or a full hot meal every night by five. Renee was nervous and tried too hard to please.

But they had prayed together and were both excited about their future.

Jonathan spent much time searching for just the right horse for his bride. After checking around, he had settled on this gentle mare. Robin stood fifteen hands tall and definitely had her own personality. She obeyed with a featherlight touch and loved to gallop at break-neck speed. She had bonded immediately with Renee. She would always come to her when called; of course, knowing a carrot or sugar cube was coming gave her great incentive. Her silky auburn mane shone with health. Riding was one of Renee's greatest blessings.

The small farm kept them both busy, but the work was reward-ing. They had developed a routine of an early breakfast and in-depth Bible study. Weather permitting, they would ride the perimeter of their property then get to work on whatever tasks were at hand. They wanted to keep the farm small so they would have free time to work their ministry. Renee had used a portion of her inheritance money to start a foundation to help battered women. They sought counsel and decided to support a shelter for women in transient. The large build-ing had a dozen efficiency apartments. They had networked with some great Christian counselors and had joined with several other churches to form an underground community for women to be res-cued from abusive situations. They had made a few mistakes, but necessary adjustments had been corrected for success. They were not involved in the day-to-day details, but they had the financial means to hire people with a level of excellence.

Renee knew that in order for the women to move on with their lives, they would need emotional healing. She had learned in her own counseling how important it was to break a soul tie from an abusive relationship. A person's mind would need to be renewed to positive thinking and Renee had learned the world's view of positive thinking and the Word of God's view of positive thinking were very different indeed. She had hired some gifted counselors and made sure the resi-dents were offered excellent Bible studies. They would also be taught daily-life skills and childcare. Computer classes were offered, as well as help with résumés and how to present and conduct an interview.

Jonathan headed up a Royal Rangers club at Living Water Church. He shared his passion and vision with Pastor Bob, and a Royal Rangers and Missionettes program was launched. Jonathan was the leader, and he had a strong team of men under him to mentor and teach the young boys. They were in the planning stage for a weekend campout on the farm.

Isaac had joined his team, and he had offered to teach the boys a series on marksmanship lessons, knot tying, and fishing. Jonathan would be giving the boys riding lessons, how to set up camp, and cook outdoors. Some of the other men at church had taken on scripture memorization, KP duty, and fire building. Eighteen boys had joined so far, and word was traveling fast.

Jonathan had designated a place for Isaac to set up a target range. Isaac had acquired two small crossbows for the boys to learn. He had mounted each bow with a scope with a simple crosshair. They had set the targets at fifteen and twenty-five yards. Each had a three-inch orange target with a black diamond in the center. These targets would allow Isaac to easily monitor each shooter and encourage them how to improve for maximum marksmanship performance.

The men had designed a badge for each activity, and at the end of the lessons, each boy would be presented with a badge for each subject, as well as a certificate of completion.

Renee was helping out with Missionettes. She didn't have a desire to be a leader, but she offered sewing lessons, and the girls responded with great enthusiasm. Angela taught them some basic cake and cookie decorations, and Grandma Esther taught them scripture memorization. The girls proudly displayed their badges they had sewn on their sashes.

* * * * *

A baptismal service was to be held at the Shenandoah River. Dale had decided to be baptized again. He had joined Living Water Church and had gotten involved in the men's ministries and a weekly Bible study. He had counseled with Pastor Bob, and even though he knew it wasn't necessary to be baptized a second time, it meant so much more to him this time around. It was an extraspecial day because little Lexus had asked Jesus into her heart, and she was getting baptized too. Although the church had a baptismal pool, in warm weather, they preferred to go to the river. The day was warm and clear, and the annual church picnic was to follow.

They were gathered at the large pavilion at the river, and the long tables were filled with food. Everyone gathered at the riverbank as Pastor Bob waded out. "Friends and loved ones, we're gathered here today to share in the baptism of our friends. These people are publicly confessing that they are followers of Christ. This act symbolizes that we are new creatures in Christ. When we go down into the water, the old man is washed away, and we come up new. When we are submerged in that water, not only are we immersed in water, we are immersed in Christ. We are buried in the likeness of His death and raised in the likeness of His resurrection. It's an honor and privilege to obey the Lord in this act of service."

There were fourteen people in line for baptism. Renee and Sharon were getting baptized, as well Mark Bishop, the mechanic Jonathan had witnessed to when he was getting his truck fixed. Jonathan had been in Tommy's Tires so many times that he had made good friends with the staff. The Lord had opened a door for him to share his faith, and Mark had responded. Jonathan was going back the following week to take them some of his homemade venison jerky. As Pastor Bob baptized each one, everyone cheered as each person came up out of the water. Lexus was the youngest of the members to be baptized, but Pastor Bob was assured that Lexus knew what she was doing.

* * * * *

The next morning, Andi found a helium balloon tied to her car antenna. It had a red heart on it but no note. *Poor Mike*, thought Andi. She drove home contemplating how she was going to tell him she couldn't see him anymore. It just wasn't fair to either of them. *He'll make someone a fine husband, but he's not for me*, Andi thought sadly. She thought long and hard if she would have regrets, but she knew in her heart of hearts that she did not love this man, and he deserved to be treasured. She drove to work at peace with her decision.

The Monday-afternoon bell rang as kids flowed outside. It had been a long day, and Andi's patience had been strung to the max. She made her way to the parking lot and found Dale leaning against her car. "Well, hey there," said Andi. "What brings you out today?"

Dale said, "Here's a sweet tea, extra ice."

Andi said, "Dale, thank you so much." He opened her car door for her. "What's this about?" She laughed.

"I know you love iced tea with a lot of ice." He smiled. "I just wanted to do something nice for you, is that okay?"

Andi nodded, feeling awkward. She got in the car, and Dale bent down and reached across her, buckling her seat belt. Andi stared at him like he had two heads. "You smell good," he said. "Drive carefully, talk to you later." He walked off but suddenly turned and called out, "Did you like my balloon?" He smiled and walked to his car.

Andi stared at him till he got in his car and drove off. She took a sip of the tea and shook her head in amazement. She laughed as she thought, *When he decides to make a move, he goes all out.*

Andi had just taken a shower and had on her favorite plush robe when the phone rang. "Hello?" she said.

"Hi, Andi, it's Dale."

Andi smiled and settled into her favorite chair.

"I'm calling to see if you'd have dinner with me Saturday evening. And just to qualify this, Andi, Lexus will not be here. My mother-in-law is taking her for the weekend. This would be a date, and I'm cooking."

Andi said, "Sure, Dale, do you need my help?"

He laughed and said, "Probably, but I want to do everything myself."

They continued chatting for over an hour. Dale was so easy to talk with. He asked her all kinds of questions that he'd never asked before. He wanted to know her favorite color and flower and her dreams for the future, but he asked in a way that was pleasurable and not invasive. His favorite color was hunter green. Hers was pale pink.

They talked about debt and the future and ministry opportunities. He asked what her taste was in furniture.

Andi said, "I've never really been able to afford to buy new, to be honest with you, so I'm not sure what my real taste is. I know what I don't like." She laughed. "I've always dreamed of having a cherry-wood four-poster bed. And I've always wanted a hope chest with a padded top covered with beautiful brocade fabric. Isn't that silly?"

He said no, he'd always wanted a jigsaw and a workshop to try his hand at woodworking. She said she'd like to learn to sew but had never bought a sewing machine. He said he wanted a ham radio to talk to people overseas. She said she'd always wanted a screened-in porch to eat outside and a gold fishpond.

Andi said, "I'd better get to sleep. What time do you want me to come over Saturday evening?"

Dale said, "How about six?"

"I look forward to it."

"Yeah, so do I. See you then. Sweet dreams, Andi." He hung up before she could reply.

Dale hung up the phone, satisfied. He had been making notes about her answers, and his head was spinning with information. "Lord, this is it. I'm making the plunge." He read over the list, making notes as he went.

The next morning after getting Lexus off to school, Dale headed for the furniture store. Before the day was over, he had made many purchases and felt great at the money well spent.

Andi reached for the doorbell at 6:00 p.m. sharp when she saw a little note taped on the door:

Andi, come right in. ☺.

She turned the knob and stepped through the door. "Dale?" she called.

He answered, "In the kitchen. Come on in."

Andi walked into the kitchen to find Dale slicing a cucumber. He had fixed spaghetti and was just finishing the salad. She could smell garlic bread in the oven. She said, "Everything smells wonderful."

He smiled and said, "Thanks, I hope you're hungry."

She replied, "I'm starving. Would you like for me to set the table?"

"No, I've already set it."

She looked at the empty table and raised her eyebrows.

"We're eating on the back deck," he said.

She opened the french doors and was shocked as the back deck had been screened in. There was a beautiful outdoor table set. She turned to him with questioning eyes. "When did you enclose this?"

"This week," he said.

She looked at him in amazement. "How did you get it done so quickly?" she asked.

"It only took two days to enclose it. It wasn't such a big job. Do you like it?"

"Oh yes, it's perfect. I love it." Andi smiled as she shook her head in amazement.

After dinner, Dale asked Andi to go into his bedroom and bring him his guitar. "I've written a new song I'd like you to hear. I'll finish loading the dishwasher while you go get it for me."

Andi went down to Dale's room and nearly fainted. The room had been painted the palest blush pink, and the old bedroom suite was gone. In its place was an exquisite cherrywood four-poster bedroom suite. Andi roamed the room taking in every detail. But a framed collage of pictures was her undoing. She slowly walked toward it. On the wall was a black framed collage of herself, Lexus, and Dale. One picture they were at the carnival, another Lexus was on Andi's lap reading in the rocker, and another was the three of them at the river.

She turned around when Dale said boldly, "I know I don't deserve you, but if you'll marry me, you'll make me the happiest man on the earth. I promise you I will do my most excellent best to never ever, ever take another drink. I will be a good husband to you, Andi, and a good father to Lexus. I'm not asking you to be my wife because you are Lexus's birth mother. I'm asking you to marry me because I can't imagine living my life without you by my side. I want to wake up to your beautiful face every morning. I want us to raise Lexus to be as godly a woman as you are. I want to spoil you and cherish you."

They were both crying.

"Say yes, Andi. Say you'll marry me."

Andi said, "Yes."

Dale shouted and grabbed her and hugged her tightly and kissed her with a passion that made her dizzy. "Let's get married tonight," he said.

When Andi saw he was serious, she contemplated. They went back out on the deck and talked.

"Why wait?" he asked. "But I don't want to cheat you out of a wedding if that's what you want," he said. "I've already had a big wedding, so of course, that means nothing to me, but this will be your big day. So if you want to buy a wedding gown, then of course, we'll do it up big, anything you want, Andi."

Andi was thoughtful for a few minutes. What did she want? It would be fun at this stage of her life to have a big wedding. She could imagine shopping for just the right gown with her mom and Abby. She smiled at the thought of Lexus being her flower girl. She had attended so many weddings in her life, and this would be her turn. She thought of having an outdoor wedding, or a wedding at Living Water, or having the ceremony at the country club. But then she looked back into his beautiful blue Irish eyes and thought of waking up beside him the next morning as Mrs. Andi O'Reilly.

Common sense won over in the end. They decided to wait and plan a little. They poured over the calendar and decided to be married on August 12, Lexus's birthday. It seemed only fitting that Lexie should get what she really wanted for her birthday: her very own mommy.

During premarital counseling with Pastor Bob, Dale realized he still had issues with bitterness over Laurie's death. They had met several times to talk about it, and the last time they met, Dale got his much-needed breakthrough.

Pastor Bob had told him that being angry with God was fruitless. "You need to learn the true nature and character of God, Dale.

He always wants what's best for you. He always loves, forgives, and desperately wants a close, loving relationship with you. You can't have the attitude toward God—'Give me what I want, or I'm not speaking to you anymore.' God isn't a man that can be manipulated. He's not moved by temper tantrums, tears, or even chanting scripture like a rabbit's foot. He's only moved by faith. And the Word tells you how to build your faith. Romans 10:17 says, 'Faith comes by hearing, and hearing by the Word of God.' It's crucial to build your faith and to surround yourself with like-minded people. You need to attend church regularly and study the Bible.

"It breaks my heart when I see people estranged from their Heavenly Father out of ignorance on their part. Their car doesn't start, so they blame God. They didn't get a job they wanted and blame God. If they only had a glimpse of His glory to know He always wants nothing but the very best for us. We have to learn to walk by faith and to take our authority as a believer. And it's also absolutely vital for our survival to forgive. Forgiveness is a choice, Dale. If we waited until our mind or heart caught up, it would never happen. It's not possible without help from the Holy Spirit.

"I want to share something I learned that is so simple yet had a profound effect on me early in my Christian walk. When I was a young pastor, a peer severely offended me, and I couldn't get past it. Over time, a root of bitterness grew deeply into my heart. It started affecting every area of my life, and I struggled to hear God and to feel His presence. A good, godly friend explained to me that forgiveness was a decision and helped me pray. He said God had forgiven me for all my sins and expected me to forgive others. He instructed me to ask God to forgive me for holding a grudge against that person and to say with my mouth that I forgave that person and that I set him free in Jesus's name.

"Then my pastor told me to imagine myself taking all that pain and unforgiveness, balling it up in a ball like a baseball, then throwing it in the river. I did that, Dale. I watched it go into the river. The river was the blood of Jesus, and when it went under, it disintegrated. Meaning, you can't go back and get it. So when the devil tries to bring it back to your mind—and you know he will—then that river can be your memorial stone where you remembered your act of forgiveness. Whenever it comes to your mind, you can bring every thought captive because you forgave that person, and it's over.

"When I got home, I got alone with the Lord and took my time praying. Anything in my life that I had even a shred of unforgiveness over, I walked through that exercise, and I'm telling you, it works, Dale. There was a huge shift in the spirit in my life, and I walked away a free man. Now I refuse to take the bait of offense. If someone hurts me, I forgive and let it go before that wily spirit can take root in my heart."

Dale took Pastor Bob's advice. After spending some significant time praying, he walked away a free man.

Pastor Bob also shared with Andi and Dale how important it was going into their marriage to make sure there was no baggage from the past. He said, "I'd like to pray with you to break all soul ties. When God created man and woman, he created them to become one flesh within the bonds of holy matrimony. That's one flesh forever throughout all their lives. When a person has an intimate relationship with someone, it creates a soul tie because that's God's plan. I know you are both strong believers in Christ and that you both have repented from any sin of the past, but let's pray now that every soul tie you've ever made in the past is broken in Jesus's name."

They prayed together and felt strengthened and renewed in their spirit and faith.

Andi said, "Pastor Bob, I can't tell you how much this means to me. Like the woman at the well, I have had a past. I don't carry that guilt any longer, but this final prayer to break soul ties is just what I needed for us to have a fresh start."

* * * * *

Dale's entire family attended the wedding. He had even invited Laurie's parents, and they graciously accepted the invitation. Andi's grandparents had invited everyone to their home for a rehearsal dinner. They sat up tables and chairs outdoors. Papaw had prayed for nice weather, very low humidity, and no gnats. They had covered the long tables with paper and had a crab feast with corn on the cob and red potatoes all cooked together in. Ron and Helene had metal washtubs filled ice and drinks, and everyone had pitched in with wonderful desserts. It was a wonderful evening of fun, food, and fellowship. Dale's parents adored Andi and credited her with all the love and support she had shown Dale when he was still in the grips of depression and alcohol.

Laurie's mother wept when she saw the beautiful photograph of Laurie that Andi had framed and hung in Lexus's bedroom. She hugged Andi tightly and said, "You don't know what this means to me."

Andi cried too and said, "Your daughter was an angel sent from heaven, Mary. She adopted my precious baby and loved her and took tender care of her. I owe everything to her, and I'll make sure Lexus will love her and that her legacy will live on."

* * * * *

The marriage was to be held at Mamaw and Papaw's farm. Nearly the entire congregation was in attendance. Andi wore a tea-length cream-colored dress with a hand-crocheted overlay. She wore her long dark hair up in a french twist with a beautiful pearl comb that was her Mamaw Esther's. Dale wore a black suit, and Lexus wore a bright-orange dress with her hair in a french braid woven with orange gerber daisies and baby's breath.

Dale played the guitar and sang to Andi as she walked down the center aisle, hay bales on each side for seating. They gathered in front of the lake with a backdrop of corn stalks, colorful mums and pumpkins, and there wasn't a dry eye as they pledged their lives to God and to each other. They had written their own vows. Dale looked Andi in the eye and said, "I pledge to be a godly leader, to provide well for my family, to be honest, true, supportive, and patient."

Andi said, "I will forgive you quickly as Christ forgave us. I will raise our daughter to be a modest, godly woman. I will do my best to submit to God and you and live my life in a way that pleases my Savior."

When Pastor Bob pronounced them man and wife, everyone shouted and applauded.

The reception was held outdoors under a huge tent. Angela baked a beautiful five-tiered wedding cake. The bottom layer was chocolate with chocolate mousse in the center. The top piece was a figurine of a man, little girl, and a woman holding hands. They had a huge punch fountain with colored lights that sprayed the punch in the air. Andi was astounded at the gift table. Everyone's generosity was staggering.

Lexus was staying a week with Abby, Isaac, and Becca while Dale and Andi went on their honeymoon. The first night, Andi wanted to stay in their own home. She told Dale she couldn't wait to sleep in their beautiful four-poster bed.

They discussed so many ideas for their honeymoon from Aruba to London to California. But in the end, they decided to stay local. They had two whole weeks for some serious R&R. They planned to canoe down the river, tour through Skyline Caverns, zip line at the State Park, go to the movies, eat out at all their favorite local restaurants, sleep late, and enjoy the wonderful breakfast at the inn.

They had made reservations at Jamestown Bed and Breakfast. Jerry and Beebee had eloped and bought a gorgeous piece of property. It had fourteen acres and overlooked the Shenandoah River. They had renovated the huge home and opened for business. They had hired someone to create a website, and with Beebee's sales and marketing experience, they were booked for months.

Before the renovation started, Jerry and Beebee had many discussions about budgeting and tithing. Jerry said, "I give generously to the church, Elizabeth, but I don't agree we have to give a full 10 percent right off the top no matter what all the time. That seems mighty rigid to me. Besides, isn't that Old Testament teaching?"

Elizabeth spent hours sharing the Word with Jerry explaining that God didn't need his money; He wanted his heart. She said, "God's Word is conditional, Jerry. He said you do this, and I'll do that. God is bound by His Word. It says in the Bible that he put His Word above His name. It takes money to further the Gospel, Jerry.

It takes money to run a church. The Lord said in Malachi 3 to test Him and try Him and that He would open the windows of heaven to pour out blessings on us when we tithe. It's the laws of reaping and sowing. I don't treat my tithe like another bill. I worship the Lord with my tithe, honey. Not just to get back, but I've also learned to name my seed. The word says we get 30, 60, and 100 percent return. I don't want 30 percent. I release my faith when I give because I know it releases God's hand to bless me. But most importantly, I tithe because I love Him and want to obey His Word."

Jerry stared at her and said, "Elizabeth, in all the years I've been a Christian, I never understood it before now. Do you know how much I adore you? Maybe you missed your calling. Maybe you should be a preacher."

Beebee laughed hard and said, "Oh, Jerry, what am I going to do with you?"

The inn house had eight bedrooms. Their personal space was the bottom floor. The middle floor had five bedrooms, and the top had the "honeymoon suite" and another large suite with adjoining rooms. Beebee and Jerry had redone all the hardwood floors, painted, papered, purchased new bedroom suites, window coverings, and bedding. Each room had a scripture verse painted on one of the walls. In the honeymoon suite, written in beautiful calligraphy, was Song of Solomon 3:4: "I have found the one whom my soul loves." There were many wonderful amenities, the best of which consisted of a hot breakfast made by Jerry. They had a menu to choose from that consisted of thick-sliced bacon, sausage patties, fried ham, steak, sausage gravy, grits, scrambled or fried eggs, omelets made to order, homemade waffles, pancakes, french toast, and fresh fruit in season. You could mix and match anything you wanted, and it could be served in the dining room or in your suite.

Andi and Dale surveyed the many gifts their family and friends had delivered to their home. They were overwhelmed with people's love, support, and generosity. "Do you want to open any tonight?" asked Dale.

Andi said, "I think I'd rather wait till we get back. I'm so worn out, and we'll need to keep notes on who gave what and deal with all the wrappings."

They agreed to select just one gift to open. Dale said, "You pick it out, babe."

Andi walked to the dining-room table and selected a very large gift with lots of gold ribbon. It was from Dale's boss. "Wow, its heavy," said Andi, laughing. Andi opened a gorgeous set of new stainless steel cookware. "Oh, Dale, look at this. What a wonderful gift. These pots and pans are such quality."

Dale said, "My boss has seen such a change in me that it's opened doors for me to witness to him. He's very happy for us, Andi, and I guess he wanted to show his support."

Andi laughed and said, "Maybe I've changed my mind about opening gifts."

Dale said, "It'll take us hours, and frankly, I have other plans for our evening, Mrs. O'Reilly."

Andi nodded, smiling warmly into his eyes. "I'm going to get out of these heels," she said, headed for their bedroom. Andi stepped into their beautiful bedroom, still marveling at what Dale had done for her. The walls were the softest, palest pink. There was a beautifully wrapped gift on their bedside table. It was from her mother. She smiled as she opened it. It was a lovely long white negligee with a matching satin robe with lace edges. It was the most feminine, beautiful nightgown Andi had ever seen. She held it up to herself and looked in the long mirror. She whispered, "Lord, I can hardly believe this day. You've led me back to my daughter. I'm so overwhelmed with Your mercy and grace in my life."

Dale and Andi were driving across Skyline Drive. The day had started off with a marvelous breakfast cooked up special by Jerry. As they rounded a curve, there was a breathtaking view of the valley. The sun had burst through the clouds, lighting up the river with a patchwork of brilliant orange and yellow. They stopped awestruck to admire the Lord's handiwork and take some pictures.

Andi said, "Dale, when are we going to tell Lexus?"

He said, "We'll pray about that, honey. The Lord will tell us when the time's right. I think we should wait until she's a little older so she can understand."

"Does she know she's adopted?"

"No. Laurie wanted to tell her, but I wouldn't let her."

Andi said, "Let's talk to Pastor Bob and see what he thinks. She's a very bright little girl, and if we handle it right, it won't upset her."

"She was so young when Laurie passed she doesn't even remember her. We can handle it so she will feel extraspecial to have been chosen." Dale paused then said, "Andi, I think God's calling me to preach." He held his breath, waiting for her reaction.

She smiled and said, "I'm not surprised at all."

"I'm not sure what to do first."

"He'll show us."

With confidence and peaceful hearts, they continued their drive through the autumn trees.

Andi and Dale strolled down Main Street enjoying the sidewalk sales. Andi and Dale were delighted as they looked at a display of framed photos for sale. A local photographer had taken pictures of all the landmarks through the valley and framed them. Andi picked up a collage frame. It was the Shenandoah River in all four seasons. "I'm buying this for Abby. She will love it. Oh look, there's another one just like it. Oh, Dale, I'd like to buy both of these. I want one too."

Dale smiled and said, "Absolutely, this will look great in our study."

They stood a long time admiring all the photographs. There was a black-and-white of the courthouse, a print of Main Street at Christmas, a photo of all the churches. The photo of Living Water Church was taken with the sun setting behind it. The church steeple was right in front of the large orange sun. The photo of Jamestown Inn was breathtaking. The inn was taken as an aerial in spring with everything in full bloom. The river was a winding ribbon below.

Dale was flipping through the aerial shots when he smiled and said, "Look at this one."

Andi was thrilled as she recognized her grandparents' farm. "Look, you can see the outbuildings and the creek." She added that to her pile. "For Christmas," she said, smiling.

Dale laughed and said, "If you can wait that long, I'll be shocked!"

There were some amazing shots of the Fireman's Carnival: children eating cotton candy, licking ice-cream cones, eating water-melon, spinning on the swings—shots of bingo and the long line at the hot-dog stand. Dale pulled out another one and said, "Check this out."

There was a picture of Miss Mazie's beautiful home restored. There was a close up that showed the sign "The Belair House." Dale had to drag Andi away, laughing.

* * * * *

Abby and Isaac were slowly drifting in the gentle current. It was a perfect day for a canoe trip. Isaac saw a red squaw vine and paddled the canoe to the bank, pulling up under a weeping willow hanging low. As they paddled underneath, the graceful limbs brushed the top of their heads. He climbed out of the boat and shinnied up the tree. He cut the vine with his pocketknife and draped it around Abby's neck. They had dressed warmly in layers as the fall air had a sharp tang that brought color to their cheeks. Abby shyly smiled at Isaac and said, "I'm sharing my testimony this coming Sunday. I've been talking to Mamaw Esther about it, and she convinced me my story needs to be told."

Isaac beamed at her and said, "I'm so proud of you. I can't wait to hear you, and I know everyone will be so blessed and encouraged."

"I'm going to tell them what happened and everything I saw. I've kept a journal. And I'm going to share with them exactly what Jesus said, 'Tell them how much I love them.' I've had a lot of time to ponder and meditate on that, Isaac. When you live a life loved, it makes all the difference. One of my home health patients adopted a baby from China. She and her husband flew to China to get the baby. When they went to the orphanage and walked into the area with dozens of cribs with tiny babies, they were met with an eerie silence. They asked why the babies weren't crying, and the workers said because the babies' cries weren't met, they stopped crying. Their basic needs were met. They propped bottles for them, but they weren't loved. There were just too many children and very few workers. They kept them from starving to death, and that was about all they could manage.

"When they picked up their daughter, she stared glassy-eyed and didn't respond. But within a couple months, she was laughing and cooing and smiling and kicking her little legs. She was living loved. And it reminded me when I was a kid. I went to school with a little girl that was extremely obese. The other kids teased and bullied her. She never had cute clothes and didn't go to the prom or take part in any of the school activities. She made straight As but hardly ever said a word. She just acted like she wanted to be invisible. I ran into her about ten years later at the grocery store, and her transformation is incredible. She is still the same size, but she was laughing and chatting and totally charming. I got to talk with her, and she had met a man that fell in love with her, and they married. She is living loved.

"How different all of our lives would be if we lived loved, Isaac. If we truly understood the depths of God's love for us, we would read His Word knowing every word was true. We would never doubt, never fear, never get mad at him or blame him when things go wrong. We would know his nature and character. We would know that God is good and wants the very best for us. We would act like the Word is true and be true and sincere worshippers. Yes, it's time for me to deliver His message that He entrusted me to give to his people. To let them know how much He loves them and longs for them to accept him as their Lord and Savior and the Lover of their soul.

"I want to go deeper with God, Isaac. I want to jump into the river of God and let His current take me where He wills."

Isaac began to sing, and soon Abby joined in harmony:

> There is a river that flows from your throne
> There is a river that flows from your throne
> For your glory let it flow through me

COME TO THE RIVER

I am your laborer, here I am, send me
There is a river
The river of God is deep and wide
Won't you step in and with Him abide
Let the living water flow over your soul
The power of His blood will make you whole

ABOUT THE AUTHOR

April Stinson Stubbs is an anointed speaker and published author with a great sense of humor and practical insight into the Word of God for everyday problems and solutions. You'll find April to be refreshingly "real" with a heart for women to be freed from emotional bondage, chase their dreams, find their place in the body of Christ and live a life with purpose and passion in Christ Jesus.

9 781098 029098